Adored by Landon

Cameron Hart

Published by Cameron Hart, 2024.

ADORED BY LANDON

First edition. January 21, 2024.

ISBN: 979-8227571946

Written by Cameron Hart.

Want a free book?

Sign up for my newsletter[1] and get your free copy of Chasing Stacy!

One look at the stunning waitress carrying the weight of the world on her shoulders, and I'm a goner. I wasn't looking for a sweet little thing with auburn hair and more baggage than I can fit on the back of my bike, but there's no going back now. She's mine. I'll prove to her I'm more than capable of handling her past and making her feel safe again.

---

1. https://dl.bookfunnel.com/7wbqvhsx8r

Connect with me!

Check out my website, cameronhart.net[2], for sneak previews on my latest projects.

Follow me on social media:

Facebook Page - facebook.com/cameronhartauthor
Instagram - instagram.com/cameron.hart.author
TikTok - tiktok.com/@author.cameron.hart
Goodreads - goodreads.com/16081533.Cameron_Hart
Bookbub - bookbub.com/authors/cameron-hart

Chapter 1

"Arnold fucking Leroy," I mutter to myself as I crank up the heat in my cruiser. The old man owns the only antique shop in town, and he's always calling the station about one thing or another. I thought I put an end to his complaints when I told him he could only dial 911 for actual emergencies. And then I had to clarify what an emergency is. Multiple times.

Instead of getting the old shop owner out of my hair, however, I seemed to have gotten more tangled up in his life. Now he filters all of his calls through my personal line at the station. Lucky me.

I suppose this is what I signed up for as sheriff of Still Creek, Minnesota. I've spent my whole life here, aside from the five-year stint I did in the military. When I came back home after catching some shrapnel in my left thigh, I decided I needed a career change. Fast forward a decade, and here I am, sheriff of my hometown.

My dedication to my career hasn't left much time for a personal life, much to the disappointment of every grandmother in town and the granddaughters they try to set me up with. I tell them the same thing every time - I'm not looking for a relationship, I'm fine on my own, and no, I don't get lonely. How can I when Arnold fucking Leroy calls me every other day?

Besides, not having to deal with Valentine's Day bullshit is reason enough to avoid relationships. Women always seem to want men to quantify their love with expensive flowers that are going to die in a week. They also want a big box of chocolates only so they can complain about how they shouldn't eat any.

Okay, so maybe I'm a little bitter and jaded from my last and only relationship, which ended eight years ago. Malory wanted more than this small town could offer. She wanted more than me. And that's just fine. She was starting to wear me out with her nagging and mind games anyway. I just don't think I'm meant to be in a relationship.

The one downside to not having a significant other or any family to speak of on the night before Valentine's Day is that I'm on call and thus have to drive to Arnold's Antiques at nine in the evening to see what the old man is throwing a temper tantrum about. He didn't say much except that there was a hooligan making trouble.

I take a deep breath as I pull into the parking lot of Arnold's store. Sure enough, Mr. Leroy himself is standing out in the bitter cold, shouting something at a hooded figure crouching in the doorway of his shop. I really, *really* don't want to deal with this right now.

When Arnold reaches out and grabs the person's arm, I jump out of my car and run toward the commotion. I may not be particularly fond of the old man, but he's going to get himself hurt if he...

Just then, Arnold drags a goddamn angel up off the dirty ground.

I hardly have time to register her breathtaking beauty before I see red. Arnold has his meaty paw wrapped around her forearm and is holding her in place, scolding her for trespassing.

I open my mouth to say something, but all that comes out is a growl. Arnold and the angel both look at me, their faces painted with shock. The woman in question has the most captivating blue eyes I've ever seen. I swear they aren't even real, they're so beautiful.

Her eyes go wide with fear and she averts her gaze. The stunning woman shrinks away from Arnold and folds in on herself, trying to be as small as possible. That heartbreaking move snaps me out of my haze.

"Let her go," I shout at Arnold, closing the distance between us.

"But she's trespass—"

"I said, let her go." My harsh tone carves through the cold night air, leaving no room for discussion.

Arnold gives the angel one last look of disdain, then grunts and drops her arm, backing away a few steps. The woman wraps her arms around her middle as if to protect herself from the world. It takes everything in me not to scoop her up and cradle her against my chest. I'll be the one to protect her from every damn thing. That's my job now, whether she knows it or not.

"She can't sleep on my stoop," Arnold mutters, putting his hands on his hips to make himself look more authoritative. "It's trespassing. I want her arrested."

A pained whimper comes from my woman, and as much as I want to kiss away her fear and promise she'll never be in this situation again, I have to be smart about this. Arnold isn't just annoying, he has the ear of a lot of councilmen and women, as well as local business owners. They are the ones who decide my career, and the election for sheriff is coming up in a few months. I don't want to piss them off, but I can't possibly arrest this pure, frightened woman.

I debate giving her a citation and a fine, but I have a feeling she won't be able to pay it, which will end up with her arrested anyway. Plus, that doesn't solve the issue that she was clearly planning to camp out here all night. That thought makes me ball my fists up and choke down my anger. Not at her, but at the fact that she could very well freeze to death out here. Where is her family? Is no one looking for her? Missing her? What was she thinking?

A plan begins to form, but I'll need her to trust me. She has no reason to, aside from the fact that she has to be feeling what I'm feeling, right? It's like I was taking shallow breaths my whole life until I saw her and filled my lungs with air for the first time. Everything about her calls to me, from her raven-colored hair to her tiny feet, covered in tattered Converse shoes. I love her from head to toe and every luscious curve in between.

"Hello? Are you going to do your job, sheriff Coleman? Or should I talk to the city council and let them know you've gone soft on crime?"

I give him a menacing look, one that makes him shiver and step back. That's right, fucker. I may be a small-town sheriff right now, but I used to be a mean motherfucker back in my Army days. It appears the slip of a woman with ethereal blue eyes brought out a protective streak in me that will ruin anyone who gets in my way from keeping her safe.

The angel presses her back against the building and tips her head up to look up at me as I approach. She's trembling, but she holds her chin up, letting me know she's not a coward. She's a fighter, my woman. I don't care what brought her here, she's mine now.

"Can I see your ID?" I ask in my most soothing voice. Making my six foot six, tatted, gruff self less intimidating isn't something I'm used to, but I'd do anything to make this woman trust me.

"I...I d-don't have it," she stutters out, the fear in her eyes hitting me square in the chest.

"Can you tell me your name, then?"

"Z...um, Mary," she lies, her voice barely a whisper. I crook an eyebrow up, letting her know I'm not buying it. "Zoe," she murmurs, looking down at her feet. Shit, is that a tear dripping down her beautiful face? I have to stick my hands in my pockets to keep myself from brushing it away and wrapping my arms around her.

"Okay, Zoe. Here's the deal. I need to take you down to the station—"

"No, please, I—"

"But you're going to be okay. I promise." She looks like she's about to protest, and then she looks like she's going to cry. Zoe swallows thickly and closes her eyes. When she opens them again, there's a quiet strength I see deep down in her core. Damn, I want to bring more of that out in her. I want her to always be brave, confident, and secure in who she is.

"About time," Arnold grumbles from a few yards away.

"Shut it," I growl as I turn Zoe around and grab my cuffs. I lean down, my lips right next to her ear. It looks like I'm reading the Miranda Rights to her, but in reality, I'm telling her my plan. "I know you have no reason to trust me," I whisper. "But I'm not going to let anything bad happen to you. You're safe, Zoe. You're safe with me."

She turns her head slightly, her eyes meeting mine. Our lips are inches apart, and as much as I want to taste her sweetness, I need to get her to safety. Zoe nods her head once before putting her hands behind her back for me to cuff them.

I place one metal cuff on her wrist, and then the other, making sure they are nice and loose so they don't dig into her delicate skin. I brush the pad of my thumb against the inside of her wrist, caressing her softly, soothingly, trying to reassure her she's under my protection now. Her hands are shaking and bright red, no doubt from the biting cold temperatures. I cup her hands in mine, squeezing them briefly to infuse some of my warmth into her freezing skin.

With a hand on her lower back, I guide Zoe over to my cruiser and help her get inside. With one last searing look, I close the door. Step one of my plan to win her over is complete.

Chapter 2

Zoe

I watch, stunned, confused, and scared out of my mind as the beast of a cop talks with the man who found my hiding spot for the night. What just happened? Am I being arrested? I'm in the back of a cop car in cuffs, so all signs point to yes. Except, the gruff, giant of a man whispered that I'm safe and I should trust him. Well, he's right about one thing - I have zero reasons to trust him or any other cop.

I was taught from an early age that the police are dangerous, evil, and always out to get us trailer trash folks. So trusting one who found me as my pathetic life is falling apart is almost laughable. Almost. The absolutely crazy thing is...I think I do. Or, I want to, at least.

The two men shake hands, though the older one who dragged me off the ground looks pissed off. The sheriff turns around, making his way back to me. He's all rough, jagged edges and brutal beauty. The lone street light shines on half of his face, casting harsh shadows over the rest of his features. His size is intimidating, but somehow I know he'd never use his strength to harm me.

The sheriff climbs into the front seat of his car, his deep, dark eyes staring at me in the rearview mirror. He cranks the heater, for which I'm very thankful. Every part of me aches, and what doesn't ache, is numb. Hot air blows across my cheeks and nose, bringing a tingling sensation with it as it thaws me out.

The ride to the police station is silent, each of us lost in thought. I have no idea what the muscled god in the front seat is thinking, but I'm trying with all my might not to have a panic attack.

I see the sign for the Still Creek Police Station up ahead, and then the imposing building beside it. Only, instead of slowing down, the sheriff keeps going. He turns left a few blocks after, then right. He weaves his way through a nice neighborhood and eventually parks in the driveway of a cute ranch-style home.

I've been on the run for more than two days straight, surviving on adrenaline and fear alone. Maybe that's where this delusion is coming from. Why would he be taking me here instead of the station?

The officer gets out of the car and opens my door, gently helping me out. I'm about to ask him why we're here, but the words get trapped in my throat. This close up, I can smell his smoky, earthy scent. It's like campfire and pine trees, yet fresh like the first snow of the year. It wraps around me, comforting me as if it's already familiar.

"Wh-what..." I begin, though my teeth are chattering too much to finish my question.

"Let's get you warmed up, okay, angel?" he murmurs. "You're safe here." He keeps saying that like he knows I don't believe it. Again, despite my better judgment, I do believe him. It must be the exhaustion.

Slowly, he turns me around so he can take the handcuffs off. I gasp when his rough, calloused hands grip my wrists, gently undoing the cuffs. His touch makes me tremble. Overwhelming warmth floods my system and a strange tightness pulls in my lower belly. I've never felt anything like it. In fact, I can't remember the last time someone's touch didn't hurt.

He drops his hands immediately, making me tremble again. Why do I feel empty and abandoned without his touch?

"Sorry," he murmurs, stepping back and motioning toward the front door. "Come inside, I have food and a hot shower. How does that sound?" I nod my head eagerly right as my stomach growls. I can't remember the last time I ate. "I'm Landon, by the way. Landon Coleman."

I nod again, stepping through the front door as he holds it open for me. His place is nice, a little messy, but cozy and lived in. It feels like home, which again, is crazy talk. I'm not sure what's happening here, but this isn't my home.

"Uh, yeah, sorry about the mess. I don't normally have company," Landon says, rubbing the back of his neck. Is he embarrassed by the takeout containers and random books strewn about? Why do I find that adorable? Here he is, taking me in for some reason, and he's worried about what I'll think about his place.

I want to say something, but I can't seem to make my vocal cords work. I'm used to keeping my mouth shut and blending into the background. Growing up, that was the only way to survive.

Landon gives me a sheepish smile, one that warms me up and draws me closer to him. This mountain of a man is a little awkward and totally endearing. Before I can dwell on the six-and-a-half-foot enigma in front of me, he turns on his heel and makes a beeline for the kitchen.

His house is an open concept, with the front door opening up to the living room and the kitchen not too far away. I can see him digging around in his cupboards for something from where I'm standing in the entryway.

My shoes are filthy and held together mostly by duct tape. My clothes are wrinkled and equally as dirty as my shoes. I haven't showered in days, and I know I have to smell horrible. I didn't have time to pack extra clothes or shoes, let alone personal hygiene stuff. A wave of self-consciousness rolls over me, and I wrap my arms around myself, wanting to disappear into the corner.

As if sensing my insecurities, Landon looks over at me, his eyes going soft. He sticks something in the microwave, then turns toward me, moving slowly so he doesn't startle me. I'm a criminal for heaven's sake, and here this cop is trying to put me at ease. It makes no sense.

"Make yourself at home, Zoe. I'll get you something to eat and then show you where the bathroom and your room is."

I stare at him, not sure I heard him right. "I'm...staying?" I whisper, searching his eyes for some sort of catch. Is this a joke? Are the cops so bored in this small town that they like to mess with the outsiders? Or worse, maybe I escaped the frying pan only to land right in the fire, so to speak. He said I'm staying here, but at what cost? I don't have any money, but maybe he wants...

"I'm not a crazy murder," he blurts out as if reading my mind. Landon dips his head and mutters something to himself. Are his ears red? Oh my gosh, I think he's blushing. "I just mean, I'm not going to hurt you. I think you've had a rough go of it, and I want to provide a safe place for you to land." It's on the tip of my tongue to ask him why he's being so nice, but a shiver runs through me, rattling my teeth. "Shit, let's get you a blanket," he mumbles, reaching for the big afghan on the back of his couch.

Landon drapes the thick, cozy blanket over my shoulders, resting his large hands on my arms for a beat before taking them away. It looks like he wants to keep holding me, but he doesn't want to make me uncomfortable. As much as I respect his restraint, I think I want him to touch more of me, with or without the blanket between us.

The microwave beeps, making me whimper like a weakling. I hate being so jumpy, and I really hate that he's seeing me like this. Not that it matters much. I'm sure this weird dream will end soon enough, and if by chance it's real, there's no way someone like him would look twice at someone like me.

Landon's brows furrow in concern, but he turns away from me to grab the food. I watch as he sets a bowl of soup down on his kitchen table and grabs crackers and a glass of water. My feet move on their own, my entire body drawn to the steaming bowl of soup.

I plop down in the chair and look at the feast before me. It's more food than I've had in a long damn time. I gulp down the soup greedily, not even bothering with the spoon. Tipping the bowl directly into my mouth, I drink it all in a matter of moments.

It's only when I set the bowl down and wipe the remnants of my meal off my face, do I realize how rude and disgusting that was. God, I didn't even say thank you or anything before devouring the food like a feral animal.

"Sorry," I whisper. "Thank you," I'm quick to follow up, showing him I have some sort of manners, even if it's been a while since I've had to use them.

Landon gives me a sad sort of smile, one I can't comprehend. Then, he stands up and proceeds to make me another bowl of soup while I finish off the glass of water in three gulps. When he sets my soup down, he immediately refills my water glass. Who is this man? Why is he being so nice and waiting on me hand and foot? I should be in a holding cell right now, not being fed by the big, sexy beast that is sheriff Landon.

This time, I manage to use my spoon and take smaller sips of water. Landon's eyes never leave mine. I can't quite place the look he's giving me. His brown eyes are intense and his jaw keeps twitching as if he's clenching his teeth. I don't think he's angry...at least not with me. Is he angry on my behalf? That doesn't make sense.

"More?" he asks once I've finished my second helping. I shake my head no, pushing back slightly from the table and resting my hands in my lap. I'm not sure what to do with myself or all the care and attention this man is giving me. "Are you sure? I've got at least twenty cans of soup in my pantry."

My lips curl up into a slight smile at the thought of Landon eating chicken noodle soup from a can every day. It's a strange feeling, smiling. I can't remember the last time I did it. I dart my eyes up to meet his gaze, surprised when I see him staring at my lips. I'm even more shocked when he returns my tentative smile, almost like making me happy makes him happy, too.

Landon clears his throat as he stands up, gathering my dishes from the table. "I'll just throw these in the dishwasher and take you on a little tour of the place. How does that sound?"

I nod my head, thankful he keeps asking me yes or no questions. I've hardly spoken more than two words to him, but he doesn't seem to mind.

Landon shows me the room I'll be staying in for the night, then motions across the hall toward the bathroom. He grabs basketball shorts and a huge t-shirt for me, along with two towels.

"Here," he says, handing them over. "I'm not sure how many towels you like to use. One for your hair and one for your...uh, well, I just wasn't sure. So...here," he says again. I can't help but grin at him. He's so dang cute, which is totally unexpected. The man is tall, broad, and covered with muscles and ink.

His hand brushes against mine as I take the clothes and towels from him. Once again, his touch is tender yet overwhelming. I'm not sure how to handle it or how to make sense of it. I've lived for so long trying to avoid others' hands on me, I don't know how to accept a touch as gentle as Landon's

"Sorry," he murmurs, withdrawing his hand. I want to tell him it's okay, that I'm not uncomfortable, I'm just confused. I want to tell him to touch me again so I can make sure I'm not crazy for craving him the way I do. But it's too late. The moment has passed. Landon shuffles from foot to foot, and then finally takes his leave, shutting the door behind him.

Twenty minutes later, I'm cleaner than I have been in weeks and snuggled up on the softest bed I've ever slept on. It even smells faintly of Landon - a hint of woods and campfire, along with a clean, cool scent. A few hours ago, I was sure I was going to freeze to death in a parking lot. Now I'm warm, clean, well-fed, and...safe. I'm safe. I don't know how long I'll be here with Landon, but I plan to savor every moment.

Chapter 3

Landon

I hardly slept a wink last night. How could I, knowing Zoe was on the other side of the wall, sleeping so close and yet too far away for my liking. I tossed and turned for hours, and then finally got out of bed, excited for the next part of my plan to woo Zoe.

I snuck out in the early hours of the morning to grab a few things from the store. When I got back, I checked in on Zoe to make sure she didn't run away or disappear. I honestly wouldn't be surprised if I made her up. She's too beautiful to be real.

But when I cracked open the door to her bedroom, she was curled up in a little ball under the blankets with just her face sticking out. She was so damn cute and cozy. I wanted to crawl in bed behind her and pull her into my arms, but that will have to wait.

Now I'm in the kitchen, looking at the groceries piled on the counter. I've never purchased Grey Poupon, fresh chives, and several other of these ingredients before, but I'm determined to make Zoe a hearty breakfast. When I set down the bowl of shitty canned soup in front of her last night, she slurped it down as if she hadn't eaten in days. Maybe she hadn't. I don't know anything about her, only that she's mine now and she deserves the best of everything. Starting right the fuck now.

When I searched "fancy breakfast" on Google, a recipe for eggs benedict with homemade Hollandaise sauce popped up. I remember having that dish a few times and liking it. Plus, it looks classy as hell and I'm hoping it will score me points with my woman. I'll show her I can provide more than just microwaved meals for sustenance.

The only thing is, I don't know how to cook. There's a reason I have twenty cans of soup and a freezer full of pre-packaged dinners. I thought I'd be alone forever, and making a meal from scratch just for myself seemed extravagant.

But now that I have Zoe, nothing is too extravagant. Nothing is too much. She should have everything she's been denied for so long. I don't know her story or anything about her, but I can tell my girl is a fighter who's seen too much shit and had to grow up far too fast. That's why she'll only ever know peace, luxury, and kindness when she's under my roof. Hopefully, I can convince her to stay forever.

Not only am I attempting to cook, but I've turned into the sappy fool I always made fun of on Valentine's day. I finally understand why roses are so expensive. There aren't enough in the whole world to show how much Zoe means to me. Like I said, sappy. Go ahead, ask me if I care.

"Okay, let's get to it," I whisper to myself as I look over the mess already spread out before me. I pull up the recipe on my phone and get to work.

First, I have to do the sauce, which requires a double boiler. Shit. The picture just looks like a normal pot. How much of a difference could it really make? I mix the ingredients directly in the pot, then set it on the stove.

On to the next step, which is grilling Canadian bacon. That's more like it. I can handle grilling. Next, I'll make the eggs. What the hell is poaching? You can poach eggs? Upon further research, poaching eggs has something to do with water and vinegar...boiling in a pan...then cracking the egg directly into—

"Shit!" I exclaim as scalding hot water splashes onto my hand. "Dammit," I mutter, seeing a few pieces of eggshell in the water, along with a big blob of broken egg. Maybe the next one will be better.

Right as I crack the second egg, smoke starts curling around the pot with the sauce in it. I grab the pot to take it off the burner, but it's too late. The sauce smells burnt, almost rancid, and it's got brown crusty pieces floating in it. Gross.

I toss the pot into the sink, only to turn around and find the vinegar egg concoction boiling over top of the shallow pan.

"Fuck!" I growl in frustration, not sure what to do or how I messed this up so badly.

Carefully removing the pan from the hot stovetop, I turn off the burner just in time to notice the Canadian bacon is burnt to a crisp. Great. The one thing I felt confident about is also ruined.

"Is everything okay?" Zoe's soft voice filters in through my banging around and cursing, instantly settling some of my restlessness.

I turn around, catching the handle of the Canadian bacon pan with my hip, sending the entire thing tumbling to the floor. Blackened pieces of leathered meat spill over the kitchen tile, one landing right in front of Zoe.

My cheeks are flushed with embarrassment. I can't remember the last time I blushed before meeting Zoe, but this woman brings out feelings and reactions I didn't think I was capable of.

To my complete surprise, Zoe starts laughing. She's not laughing at me, I can tell, more at the situation. I look around the kitchen, noticing what a disaster zone it really is. I can't help but throw my head back and laugh right along with her.

"I wanted to make you breakfast," I finally say when I catch my breath. "But it turns out I don't know how to cook."

Zoe gives me a shy little smile, one that melts my heart. She bends down and picks up the piece of Canadian bacon that landed at her feet and tosses it in the trash can before picking up the other pieces. "It looks like it was going to be a feast," she says softly as she continues to clean up.

I notice she only has on the shirt I gave her last night. It's practically a dress on her, hanging past her knees, but Christ does she look good in my clothes. I clear my throat and try to think of anything other than sliding my hands up her thighs to see if she's wearing any panties.

"You don't have to clean, this is my mess," I tell her as I grab paper towels and start sopping up all the spills.

"I don't mind." Zoe smiles again, her pink lips curling up slightly as her blue eyes meet mine. "But you'll have to tell me what it is I'm cleaning up," she teases.

I'm momentarily struck dumb by her presence. Last night she was so skittish and wary. I can't blame her in the least, but I love seeing her with her defenses down. It gives me hope.

"Eggs benedict," I answer once I find my voice. I have to turn away from her before I get a fucking hard-on. That's not the way to win over my woman. I'll have to be careful with her. She's so precious to me already, and I'd never want to make her uncomfortable or pressure her to do anything.

But God, when she eventually trusts me with her body, I have so many plans for her. I'll spread her out on the table and have her for breakfast every morning. I'll feast on her juicy little cunt until she screams my name and begs me to fill her up. I'll fuck her so damn hard, so damn deep, she'll know she's mine forever.

Not helping, I chastise myself.

"That's an ambitious meal to make," Zoe says, her tone soft and gentle as she scrubs off the stovetop. I feel like a big clumsy oaf next to her, but she doesn't seem to mind.

"I wanted you to have something nice to wake up to," I say with a shrug. Taking another look around my jacked up kitchen, I can't help but chuckle. "A big swing and a miss, huh?" I joke.

When I turn around, Zoe is starting right at me with tears in her wide, blue eyes. My heart feels like it's being ripped out of my chest. What did I say? What did I do? Am I the reason she's crying? Shit, shit, *shit*!

"You...wanted me to have something nice?" she whispers, like she can't believe it's true. I nod my head, afraid I'll make her cry if I say anything. "But...why?"

Without thinking, I reach out to her, but stop as soon as I see her flinch away. Goddamnit, whoever hurt her will pay.

"Because you had a rough night, and I assume a rough couple of days," I say softly, shoving my hands in my pockets to keep from reaching out again. "I thought you could use some food that didn't come in a can," I say with a smirk, hoping to lighten the mood.

Zoe rewards me with a tiny smile. I'll take it. I'll take whatever pieces of her heart she gives me.

We work in a comfortable silence, Zoe washing dishes while I dry them. She sweeps and I follow up with the mop. Before long, the place is looking good as new. Better even, since I'm here with Zoe.

"Oh!" I exclaim, remembering the other things I got for this morning. "I have something else for you. Wait right here." Zoe tilts her head to the side, giving me the most adorably confused look. "I promise it doesn't involve cooking," I say with a wink.

Before she can question me any further, I dart out of the room, hoping my next surprise will end better than my first one.

Chapter 4

He wanted me to have a nice breakfast.

For the hundredth time since meeting Landon, I'm overwhelmed by his kindness. I don't know how to react, how to show him my gratitude. I grew up knowing I was trash. I was told that for as long as I can remember. *You came from trash and you'll always be trash.* I learned early on that people don't treat trash very nicely.

But I don't feel like trash when Landon looks at me. I feel precious. It's an entirely foreign concept to me. He looks at me like I'm his whole world. His gaze is somehow both fierce and tender. The man is a contradiction, that's for sure. He's got this big heart and beautiful soul all wrapped up in delicious muscles and swirling black ink. It'd be a dream come true to have him all for myself, but that will never happen. Especially if he finds out trespassing is the least of the crimes I've committed recently.

Landon interrupts my downward spiral when he steps back into the kitchen, holding something behind his back. A nervous smile plays at his lips, making my heart melt. No one has ever cared enough about me to want to make a good impression.

"Here," he says rather ungracefully, handing me a beautiful bouquet of red roses and a giant heart-shaped box of chocolates.

I don't even know how to process what's happening right now. I'm literally struck dumb, completely confused as to why he's giving me these things.

"I...these are for me?" I whisper, unable to believe it.

"Of course," he says with an encouraging smile. "A beautiful woman deserves beautiful flowers and chocolate on Valentine's Day."

Me? Beautiful? My brain rejects that idea immediately, moving on to the next part of his sentence. "I didn't even know it was Valentine's Day," I murmur, reaching out for the bouquet with shaking hands.

Bringing the roses up to my face, I inhale their perfumed scent. I think it's the first time I've ever smelled fresh flowers, let alone expensive roses.

"Don't forget the chocolates," Landon says excitedly. I have no idea why he's trying to impress me. Surely the Greek god of a man has no trouble getting any woman he wants.

I take the huge box of chocolates, setting them on the counter and opening the lid. Inside are all kinds of fancy treats in an assortment of flavors. I've never had anything so extravagant before. I don't realize I'm crying until a tear drops onto one of the decadent chocolate truffles.

"Shit," Landon mutters. "I-I...what's wrong? Did I do something to upset you? I thought flowers and chocolate were a safe bet, but...are you allergic? Gluten-free? Does chocolate have gluten? Or the roses—"

"I love them," I say on a shaky breath, not wanting him to spiral even more. God, he's so sweet and for some reason, he's bent on winning me over. To what end, I'm not sure, but I don't have the capacity to process any of that right now. "No one has ever given me anything before."

Landon lets out a huge breath, clearly relieved that he's not at fault for my tears.

"I find it hard to believe such a gorgeous woman has never received gifts on Valentine's Day."

There it is again. *Gorgeous.* "No, I mean...no one has ever given me anything, like, ever." Why did I say that? God, I'm pathetic. I clap my hand over my mouth, physically stopping more words from coming out. At this rate, I'll spill all of my secrets by noon, and I can't afford that.

Out of the corner of my eye, I see Landon's hand moving slowly, as if not to startle me. I let him loop his fingers around my wrist, gently pulling my hand away from my mouth. He laces our fingers together as he takes a step closer to me.

He doesn't say anything, but the look he gives me speaks volumes. I see such tenderness and concern in his deep brown eyes, but not pity. He sees me, truly sees me, and in this moment, I feel safe and accepted in a way I never knew was possible. I'm not my past, I'm not the dirty kid from the trailer park, I'm not my stepdad's punching bag. I'm just...me. I don't even know who I am, but somehow Landon does.

The moment becomes too much for me. The gifts, the sweetness, the way his calloused thumb is gently rubbing over my knuckles...I'm feeling things I've never felt before and I'm suddenly hit with a wave of sadness, knowing this will all come to an end soon.

I pull my hand out of his and take a step back. The look he gives me nearly breaks my heart. Is he really as affected by me as I am by him?

"Sorry," he murmurs softly, taking a few steps back and shoving his hands in his pockets as if he needs to restrain himself from touching me again.

The thing is, I want him to. At least, my body does. I crave his attention, his skin on my skin, his earthy, smoky scent wrapping around me. But my mind is still reeling, my heart still aching and confused at the sudden turn my life took a few days ago.

"No, I..." I don't know what to say, how to tell him what I want. I start to reach out for him, but my courage fades and I drop my hand at my side before looking down at my feet. "Thank you," I whisper. "The flowers are beautiful."

"You're beautiful," he says immediately, making me blush. If he doesn't stop saying that, I might just believe him. Landon clears his throat and wipes his hands on his jeans, turning around to fiddle with something on the counter. "Breakfast didn't work out as planned, but I can make a mean slice of toast." He looks at me over his shoulder and grins, breaking the tension and heaviness in the air.

"I just so happen to love toast," I say with a little more confidence. "Especially when paired with chocolate."

The rest of breakfast goes much better, with Landon doing most of the talking. He tells me about growing up in Still Creek, how he was a little hellion in high school but cleaned up his act after his grandma, the woman who raised him, died unexpectedly when he was eighteen. Landon enlisted in the Army the day after her funeral, leaving everything he knew behind to serve his country.

I was shocked and saddened when he told me about his injury and what brought him back to Still Creek. I listen to his deep, smooth voice, like honey over gravel, as he talks about his job and the characters that make up this small midwestern town.

"So, listen," Landon says as we finish clearing off the table. "I have to go into the station for a bit this morning, and I'll be on call for the rest of the day, but I'd like you to stay."

"Here?" I ask, stupidly. Landon smiles, his kind eyes putting me at ease once more.

"Yeah. I have Netflix, Hulu, HBO, all that stuff. I'll get my laptop out, too, if you need to get online for anything. I have soup for lunch, as you probably know," he says with a wink. "And I'll pick up dinner on the way home."

"But...why?"

Landon stops drying off the last of the dishes and turns to face me, searing me with another meaningful look. We're close enough that I have to tip my head back to meet his gaze. His warm breath skates across my skin, sending a shiver of pleasure down my spine that lands between my thighs. My core clenches up, releasing an unexpected wave of arousal. He's the only person who's ever elicited that response in me.

"One day, you won't doubt my intentions," he whispers. "One day, you'll see what I see."

"What do you see?"

His eyes bore into mine, pleading with me to believe him. "I see forever, right here with you." My eyes go wide, unable to comprehend his words. Slowly, so slowly, he leans forward, brushing the softest, sweetest kiss onto my forehead. "Happy Valentine's Day, Zoe," he whispers before stepping away.

I'm still gaping at him as he retreats into his room to get ready for work, but I quickly snap out of it and distract myself by putting the dishes away. He can't be serious, right? What could someone as strong, handsome, and kind as Landon possibly see in someone like me?

Chapter 5

Landon

I've been lying in bed, awake for hours now, preparing for another shit night of sleep. Zoe has been staying with me for three days, and this will be the fourth night of very little sleep. It's worth it to know she's safe, but it's killing me to not be able to hold her all night and kiss away the sadness and fear I sometimes see lingering in her beautiful blue eyes.

Despite my big, bumbling self, Zoe seems to be warming up to me more and more all the time. I've never been this tongue-tied or awkward around anyone before, but then again, I've never met anyone like Zoe. Every interaction between us binds her closer to my heart.

My angel hasn't talked about why she was sleeping outside in the dead of winter, but she's given me little pieces of herself. I know Zoe is twenty years old, thirteen years my junior. That should probably turn me off, but I find it only makes me more protective of her. I've learned she likes tea, classic rock, and reading anything she can get her hands on. I've also learned she likes to draw, but for some reason, she's embarrassed about it. One day soon she'll trust me not just with her safety, but her hopes and dreams as well. Whatever they are, I'll make them come true.

I've somehow managed not to touch her since the morning of Valentine's day almost seventy-two hours ago. It might not seem like a lot of time, but I swear to God I'm already addicted to everything about her. I may have only barely touched her hand and kissed her forehead, but I still feel her soft, warm skin on my lips and fingertips.

I swipe my thumb over my bottom lip, reliving that brief moment of contact like a fucking schoolgirl with a crush. That's what she's reduced me to. Only it's so much more than a crush. I told her that morning I see forever with her, and I meant it.

Rolling onto my back, I try to get in a more comfortable position, but I know it's pointless. I won't get a solid night's sleep until she's in my arms. Closing my eyes briefly, I take a calming breath. Then I hear my bedroom door creak open.

I swear Zoe is standing in the doorway, her frame silhouetted by the soft light coming from the hallway. Surely I must be dreaming.

My angel makes her way closer to the bed, her tentative steps and shallow breaths the only sounds in the room. I let my eyelids flutter closed, not wanting to scare her away. I have no idea what she's doing here, but I want her to be in control of the situation. I'll be whatever she needs, all she has to do is ask.

She pulls the covers back on the empty side of my king-sized bed and carefully climbs in. The bed shakes slightly with each movement, and I hold my breath, waiting for whatever's coming next. Zoe scoots closer and closer until I can feel the heat of her body right next to mine.

My heart hammers in my chest so forcefully I'm worried she might hear it and run away. To my complete shock, Zoe slips her soft little hand in mine. My sweet girl melts into my side, resting her cheek against my bicep. After a few moments, Zoe laces our fingers together and snuggles up closer to me.

I squeeze her hand slightly, unable to stop myself. Zoe tenses, gasping quietly. "Is this okay?" she whispers.

"This is perfect," I whisper back, pressing a kiss on the crown of her head. My angel relaxes once again, and I do, too. I want to pull her into my arms and wrap myself around her, but this will have to do. She's letting me in and telling me without words she's comfortable with my touch. That means the world to me. It gives me hope she'll trust me with her mind, body, and soul soon enough.

***

I slowly blink my eyes open, unsure what woke me. The first golden rays of morning sunlight peek through the edges of the curtains, letting me know it's still early.

More awareness floods my body, and I look down to see the most gorgeous sight. Zoe is sound asleep and wrapped around me like a spider monkey. I'm on my back while she's draped over my chest, her head tucked under my chin. My dick springs to life when I realize she's straddling me, her hips gently rocking up and down.

Jesus, she has no idea I'm about to come in my goddamn pajama pants. My cock twitches, growing harder by the second. I'm about to adjust her so I don't scare her away by being a creep, but then I hear the sweetest, sexiest little moan fall from her lips.

"Landon," she whimpers, her thighs tightening around my hips. I tip my head back, swallowing down a growl. Zoe rubs her pussy against me, burying her head into the side of my neck. She's still asleep, but fuck, she's having a sexy dream about me. That thought has the fucker in my pants leaking precum like a faucet.

I want to do so many things to her tight little body, but I'd never take advantage of her. My fists clench at my sides, shaking with the need to touch her. It physically hurts not to grab her hips and grind her hot little cunt against my cock or tangle my fingers in her hair and tilt her head up so I can claim her lips.

But this is about her comfort and pleasure.

I bite the side of my cheek and take measured breaths as this sexy as hell woman rubs herself against me, moaning softly in her sleep while she uses me to get off. Fucking Christ, my muscles tense and my whole body trembles, the need to flip her over on her back and sink into her eager pussy nearly choking me.

My aching dick swells up even more when Zoe scrapes her teeth down my throat and moans loudly. I feel her damp heat through the fabric of my thin cotton pants. I can tell the only thing she has on is the oversized t-shirt I gave her a few days ago to wear as pajamas. No underwear.

My hips jerk, thrusting up on their own when I feel her pussy lips spread around my thickness. Zoe whimpers as she grinds down on my barely covered cock. She's fucking soaking the material with her juices.

I fist the sheets in my hands, bowing my back off the mattress, the pain of restraint jacking up my heartbeat and making me sweat.

"Landon," she moans again, her fingernails digging into my sides for leverage as she grinds herself on top of me. "Yes, yes, Landon, Landon..." Her whimpers grow louder, more desperate as she reaches her peak.

Right before her orgasm hits, Zoe's eyes flash open, searing me with her lust. She looks surprised, confused, and so fucking turned on it hurts.

"Come for me, angel," I whisper.

Zoe leans forward, her lips meeting mine in a frantic kiss. I slip my tongue inside her mouth, tasting her for the first time. Goddamn, she's sweeter than any chocolate, more delicate than any rose. And sexier than any woman I've ever seen.

Her body grows tight, her muscles taut and trembling. I nip at her lips, pulling her bottom one through my teeth before diving back in for another taste.

Zoe unravels so beautifully for me, gasping and moaning her ecstasy into my mouth as she rolls her body on top of mine. Unable to hold back any longer, I slide my hands up her smooth thighs, gripping her hips and holding her still as I grind against her, scraping her clit with each thrust.

My angel tears her mouth away from mine, arching her back as she comes again, her climax devastating her little body. I hold her close as aftershocks rattle through her, whispering soothing things into her ear before kissing her cheek.

Finally, Zoe goes limp in my arms. I love feeling the weight of her body on top of me, her soft curves melting into the hard slats of my muscles, her shallow breaths tickling my skin.

"Oh my God, I'm…I'm so sorry, I don't know what came over me."

"Shh, there's nothing to apologize for," I assure her, combing my fingers through her hair. "You're so beautiful, Zoe. That was the best way to wake up."

She pops her head up from my chest, giving me a shy smile. Her cheeks are stained red, partially from her orgasms and partially from embarrassment. I kiss the tip of her nose, making her giggle. Closing my eyes, I savor the sound. I know we have a long way to go still, but this morning was the sweetest, most precious gift she could have given me.

Zoe leans forward, giving me the barest hint of a kiss before curling up on my chest once more. "Thank you," she whispers. I know she's thanking me for more than just this morning.

"You never have to thank me for taking care of you, angel."

"I'm no angel," she murmurs, her voice heavy with sleep.

"You're my angel," I whisper, rubbing soothing circles on her back. She's asleep within minutes, making me chuckle. She's mine. And the best part is, I think she's starting to realize it, too.

Chapter 6

Zoe

I've only known Landon for a week, but I already know he's ruined me for all other men. He's not only patient, attentive, and sweet, he's ridiculously, mouthwateringly sexy. And damn does he know how to make me come.

There weren't many times I felt safe enough in my stepdad's trailer to touch myself like that, and when I did, it was nothing, *nothing* compared to what we did a few days ago. God, I literally mauled him in my sleep, and he went with it, showing me how much pleasure my body can handle.

I was so embarrassed at my actions once I came out of my blissed-out state. Landon didn't let me spiral for long, though. He held me and gave me the gentle reassurance I didn't know I needed. Then again, that's how he's been with me from the very beginning. The strong, stoic sheriff has given me everything without me having to ask.

It's more than just a roof over my head and food in my belly. Landon has won over my trust in such a short amount of time. I should be warier of him, considering his imposing stature and position of power, but I know he'd never hurt me. From day one, he's only ever shown me kindness and understanding. Landon provided a safe place for me, no questions asked. If anything, he should be warier of me.

I shove that thought aside and focus on the dinner I'm cooking for Landon to thank him. And also, maybe to seduce him. He's been the perfect gentleman since the morning he gave me two incredible orgasms. We didn't talk about it, but I've been sleeping in his bed ever since. Unfortunately, he hasn't touched me the same way, or hardly at all. I can tell he wants to, hell, I can see the evidence of his arousal pretty much any time he's in the same room as me.

I know he's giving me space to heal and to process, even if he has no idea why or what I've been through. I respect his restraint and his thoughtfulness, but that's not what I want or need. I need him, all of him. I crave his rough hands on my smooth skin, those soft yet demanding lips on mine. He's created a gnawing ache in my core, one I know only he can fix.

The timer for the pesto chicken goes off, startling me from my thoughts. Landon wasn't kidding when he told me he can't cook. The man has somehow been living off of takeout and frozen dinners. How someone can eat that crap and still have a body carved out of marble, I'll never understand. Luckily for him, I'm actually a halfway decent cook. I had to learn fast, otherwise, I'd face the wrath of my stepdad.

A shiver runs down my spine at the visceral memory of him throwing a plate of spaghetti across the room because the noodles were undercooked. It barely missed my head. The next time he did it, I wasn't so lucky.

"What smells so amazing?" Landon says as he walks in the front door. The ghosts from my past scatter and retreat to the dark corners of my mind at the sound of his voice. I want him to banish them for good, but that would require spilling my secrets.

"Chicken pesto with cheese ravioli," I tell him with a smile.

I love it when he comes home from work. Landon always gives me this goofy, adorable grin as soon as he spots me. It makes me feel so wanted, so cherished, like he's missed me every moment we've been apart. Lord knows I always miss him when he's not around. It's dangerous how much I crave him, but we're inevitable. I couldn't stop this pull between us if I wanted to, and I don't want to. And tonight is the night I prove it to him. Tonight is the night I'm going to give him my virginity.

"You made all that?" he asks, stepping into the kitchen. Landon pulls me into his arms, cradling me against his chest. I melt into his embrace, breathing in his familiar clean yet smoky scent. It's a contradiction, just like the rest of him. One I'd love to spend the rest of my life trying to figure out.

"Yup," I confirm, sliding my arms around his torso and clinging to him with all my strength. Hugging is pretty much the most physical contact he's allowed since that mind-blowing morning, so I soak up his touch for as long as I can. Hopefully, I'll be getting more of it soon.

Landon tries stepping away from me as soon as I feel his thick dick swell up and harden. I won't let him get away from me this time, though. Reaching down, I slide my palm over his cock, rubbing gently at first, and then harder when he groans and jerks his hips.

"Fuck," he growls under his breath, the sound rough and almost pained. "Zoe..."

I cut off whatever he was going to say by lifting up on my tiptoes and pressing my mouth to his while squeezing the intimidating bulge in his pants. Landon groans, tangling his fingers in my hair and tilting my head to the side. He deepens the kiss, sliding his tongue against mine in desperate strokes.

His other hand squeezes my hip and then grips my ass, pulling me closer so he can grind against me. I whimper into his mouth, causing him to groan and tighten his hold.

Landon tears his lips away from mine, his breath coming out in harsh pants. "You can't do that to me, angel," he whispers, resting his forehead on mine.

"Why?" I ask innocently as I rub my body against his. I feel his muscles tense and flex against me as my nipples scrape across his chest. Even through the fabric of our clothes, I'm sure he can feel my hardened peaks.

"You know why," Landon groans, tipping his head back as his hands roam over my body, caressing me and sending shivers up and down my spine.

"Tell me," I whisper, kissing the side of his neck. I have no clue what I'm doing, but it seems to be working.

The big sexy beast looks down at me, heat and hunger pouring from his gaze. It's a palpable thing, his desire. I feel it drip down my skin, coating me in anticipation, and setting my nerves on fire.

I feel his labored breathing against the shell of my ear, making me whimper and fist his shirt, drawing me closer to him.

"You want me to tell you all the filthy fucking thoughts I have about you?" he growls softly, slipping his hands beneath the hem of my shirt. I nod my head, gasping at his teasing touch. Landon trails his fingers up my bare back and around to my front, cupping my breasts as he whispers dirty things into my ear. "God, Zoe, I want my lips on every inch of you. I want you to come on my fingers, my tongue, my big fucking cock. I want to sink inside your tight little pussy over and over until my name is the only word you know. And these tits..." Landon leans back slightly, lifting my shirt over my head and revealing my breasts to him. "Jesus, I'm gonna fuck them, too."

"Yes," I breathe out, arching my back so he can have better access. Landon wastes no time sucking on one aching nipple and then the other. "I want it, I want you, Landon."

"Say it again," he grunts, licking a path up my throat and scraping his teeth against my pulse point.

"I want you, Landon."

"How do you want me, angel?"

"However you'll have me."

Landon slips one hand under the waistband of the boxers I'm wearing, cupping my ass and squeezing it in a punishing hold. "I'll have you right here on the kitchen table," he growls. I whimper when he slides two fingers through my folds, drawing slow circles around my pulsing entrance from behind. "I'll have you bent over the couch," he grunts, pushing just the tip of one large finger inside me. "So fucking wet and tight for me. Shit, I'll have you anywhere and everywhere. I'll fuck you up against the wall, spread you out in front of the fireplace, sink into your little cunt underneath the stars."

I'm breathing so hard I might just pass out, but it'd be worth it. "I always pictured my first time in a bed," I whisper. He freezes, his finger still lodged inside my throbbing channel. I worry I said the wrong thing, that maybe I should have kept my virginity a secret, but it's too late now. It's not like he wouldn't find out eventually anyway.

Landon groans before ghosting his lips down the side of my neck and thrusting two fingers inside me. "You're saying this juicy little pussy is going to be all mine? Only mine?" I nod as a wave of wetness spills out of me, coating his hand. "Say it," he demands.

"Only yours."

Before I know what's happening, Landon has me in his arms. He sets me down on the counter, stepping between my spread legs. My heart is pounding in my chest, the frantic beat mirrored in my clit. I squirm in his arms, feeling restless and achy.

Landon chuckles darkly before placing open-mouthed kisses over my breasts, my collarbone, and up my neck. I moan into his mouth as he kisses me with fire and fury. His hands roam all over my body, eventually landing on my hips, where he begins tugging the last piece of fabric I'm wearing.

"Lay back, baby," he murmurs. "Let me taste what's mine." Landon spreads one large hand over my stomach, urging me to lay down on the counter. I obey, lifting my hips so he can take the boxers off. "God... Zoe..."

My core clenches, knowing he's staring right at me, at my most intimate, private place. Landon looks more than hungry. He looks fucking feral.

He grabs my hips and jerks me so my ass is on the edge of the counter. He digs his nose between my legs, parting my folds and inhaling deeply. My thighs shake as he slowly licks me from bottom to top, rolling his tongue against my clit and making me moan.

The next thing I know, Landon slings my legs over his shoulders before shoving his face in my pussy.

"Oh! Landon, God, I..."

My senses are flooded, overwhelmed in the best way possible. His tongue darts in and out of my entrance, his nose circles my clit, and the stubble on his chin tickles the insides of my thighs. When he growls into my pussy, I gush for him, making him growl again.

Landon lifts his head and I stare down at him between my legs. He's covered in my juices, the sight sending shivers of pleasure echoing around my body. His hands hold me steady when my hips jerk involuntarily, trembling with pleasure.

I feel him suck on my folds, first one side, and then the other. Landon turns his head and nips at my inner thigh before kissing the sting away. He gives the same attention to my other thigh and then licks up my slit. He's avoiding my clit, licking me everywhere except where I need him most.

"Fucking delicious," he groans, staring right at my core. My walls pulse under his scrutiny. "Jesus, angel, you're throbbing for me."

"Please." I try finding my voice, but I know it's barely a whisper.

Landon grins and then dips his head, working me up again. My juices trickle down my slit, tickling me and causing me to cry out. Landon's tongue follows the trail, licking my ass and causing me to jump. He chuckles and resumes his attack on every single part of me.

My head falls down to the counter as I grab his hair, riding his face, needing to find release for the orgasm he's been teasing me with for what feels like hours. He sucks my clit into his mouth, rolling it between his teeth, and I break.

"Landon!" I shout. He licks me through my orgasm, sending me up and over, again and again. "God, I can't...I can't stop," I cry out, gripping his hair.

I tremble as I come, pleasure rolling through my body and blocking out all thoughts. All sights. All sounds. The world disappears and there's nothing left but my body gushing for him as he demands my orgasm.

Every bit of strength has been wrung out of my bones, and now drips down Landon's face. He stands up and leans over me, kissing me long and deep. I taste myself on him, which is so much hotter than I thought it would be. He tries to pull away, but my mouth follows his. I bite his soft lips and lick my juices off the tip of his nose.

"Fuck," Landon growls, gathering me up in his arms and kissing me wildly. "You like that? Like when I kiss both of your lips?"

"Yeah," I gasp before he bites my shoulder.

"Jesus Christ, I want to devour every inch of you."

"Yes, please. Do that to me."

"What about dinner?"

"We can heat it up," I practically whimper, not wanting to stop for a single second, even for the delicious food I prepared.

"But you worked so hard on it," he counters, though he sounds just as pained at the thought of stopping as I am.

"I only made it to seduce you, but I think I managed to do that without the food," I tease.

Landon makes some sort of strangled sound in the back of his throat and then throws me over his shoulder.

"Landon!" I shriek, surprised by his caveman move. He grunts, completing the whole caveman routine. I giggle and then shriek again when he tosses me down on the bed.

The way he's looking at me as I spread my legs and offer him everything says it all. Once he claims me, I'll be his. I only hope he'll still want me when my past inevitably catches up to us.

Landon lifts his shirt over his head, revealing the sculpted muscles of his chest and torso. Every inch of him is hard, including the monster trying to break free from the prison of his pants. I watch with rapt attention as he unbuttons his jeans and slides them down his legs along with his boxers. His huge, hard cock juts out, making my mouth water.

God, he's so… brutally beautiful. Landon's intense eyes capture mine, the need I see in them matching my own. I bite my bottom lip and tilt my hips up, wanting him inside me so much it hurts.

My big, beastly man fists his cock, giving himself rough strokes as he looks over my body. I thought I'd be self-conscious about Landon seeing me naked, but watching his dick grow even more, clear liquid dripping from the tip, puts all of my doubts to rest.

With a final jerk, Landon lets go of his throbbing thickness and stalks toward the bed, crawling up my body and nestling himself between my legs. Bracing himself over me with his hands on either side of my head, Landon bends down and kisses me soundly. He breaks the kiss and puts his weight on one hand, cupping my face with the other.

"Are you ready, love?"

"Yes," I answer immediately.

"Are you sure?"

"Yes, please, Landon. I want this. With you. I…" I trail off and turn my head.

Landon gently guides my face back toward his. "Eyes on me, angel. You what?"

"I want to feel you inside me," I confess. "Make me yours completely."

He groans and bites my bottom lip before kissing away the pain. "Anything you want. I'll give you all of me." He lines up his huge cock to my entrance and pushes a few inches inside. "Relax, angel. Let me into this perfect little pussy."

He kisses me, long and slow, as he thrusts a little deeper. I whimper as he stretches me and fills every inch of me.

"Breathe, baby. It'll only hurt for a minute."

He dips his head to my neck and nips at the skin. I feel him tear through me, the pain spreading throughout my body. I grip his biceps, my nails biting into his skin. Landon swallows my cry and stays still, deep inside me. Tears slide down the side of my face, but I keep breathing through the pain.

"I'm so sorry, love." His eyes are full of remorse as he kisses away my tears. "I promise it'll get better. I'll make this good for you." I nod and he pulls back out, dragging his huge length along the walls of my pussy before pushing back in again. "Fuck, you feel incredible. You were made for me, only me. God*damn*, Zoe."

He sets a steady rhythm and soon the pain subsides, giving way to an incredible feeling of being full. Full of Landon. Finally connected to him in every way, as close as we can possibly be. I start to lift my hips with his, keeping up with his thrusts.

"Jesus Christ, you're incredible. Are you okay?"

"Yes..." It comes out more like a moan.

Landon grins and picks up the pace. Wrapping my arms around his neck, I pull him in for a kiss.

"More," I moan. He growls and sits back on his heels, throwing one of my legs over his shoulders. "Oh, yes, Landon..."

The new angle takes him deeper, stretching me in the most delicious way. He brings his thumb down to my clit and begins rubbing circles around the sensitive ball of nerves. My legs start shaking and I know I'm close. I'm almost afraid of how big this orgasm is going to be.

"That's it, angel. I want to feel you come all over my big cock. I want to feel you squeeze me and milk the cum from my balls. Do you want that? Want me to fill you with my cum?"

I can only whimper at this point.

I thrust my hips up and take him deeper, chasing my pleasure and his. I feel something huge barreling through me, threatening to consume me completely. I'm right on the edge, the delicious tipping point. My muscles strain and tense, trying to hold on to my last shred of control.

"Come for me, baby. Fucking come all over me."

I scream, actually *scream* his name as my pussy gushes and pulses pleasure like I've never known throughout my entire body. I come so hard I see white. I forget to breathe, completely enraptured by the sensations taking over my body.

"That's it, angel. I'm coming, with you, love." I feel his cock grow impossibly bigger before shooting rope after rope of his hot, sticky cum inside of me. I feel it hit me deep, setting off another orgasm.

Landon snarls into the side of my neck, rutting into my still-spasming cunt. Our combined orgasm lasts forever, both of us pulsing and thrusting together as one. Wet, sloppy noises fill the room and the smell of sweat and sex surrounds us. Every one of my senses is on overdrive as I drink it all in.

I cry out as a final, intense orgasm shoots through me, ripping me apart before stealing my strength and the breath in my lungs. Landon grinds his half-hard cock into my core, feeling my orgasm with me.

When I'm completely spent, Landon sets my leg back down on the bed and collapses on top of me, quickly rolling over and dragging me over his chest. We're both sweaty and panting.

"Are you okay, angel?"

"That was everything," I whisper.

He smiles down at me and wraps me in his arms. "*You* are everything, love. That was amazing."

I curl up on his chest, letting this sweet, sexy man hold me and whisper promises of forever in my ear. The moment is so pure, so perfect, I almost believe we can overcome anything that comes our way. Almost.

Chapter 7

Landon

If I wasn't sure before, I definitely am now. I love Zoe more than I thought possible. It's about time she knows it, too.

Looking at her sweet angelic face as she sleeps peacefully makes my chest grow tight. I remember the first time I saw her, the pain and fear radiating off of her little body as she cowered away from Arnold.

Right now, though, my angel looks so serene. Pride swells up from deep inside me knowing I provided a safe place for her to land after whatever the hell she's been through. We haven't talked much about her past, but I haven't pressed her on the topic. I know she'll tell me in her own time. Besides, it doesn't matter. Whatever she's afraid of, whatever life she left behind, she's mine now. I'll protect her and provide for her always.

Zoe turns toward me, rolling on her side and sighing so sweetly. I bend down and brush the lightest hint of a kiss on her forehead, savoring the contact of her skin against my lips. When I lean back, my beautiful angel blinks her eyes a few times before looking up at me. A slow, soft smile spreads across her lips, accompanied by the most adorable blush.

I rub my nose against hers, then angle my head so I can kiss her for real. Zoe responds immediately, pressing her body closer to mine and nibbling on my bottom lip.

Just like that, my dick springs to life, adrenaline coursing through me and spiking my lust for her. When my angel slides her hand down my bare chest and wraps it around my cock, I lose my damn mind.

Flipping her on her back, I gather her hands up in one of mine, pinning them above her head. I nuzzle into the side of her neck, dragging my lips up her throat and nipping at her pulse point. Zoe whimpers for me, the sound making my muscles tense and my hips flex.

I grind my hard as fuck dick against her center, letting her feel the way she affects me.

We're both still naked, thanks to the several times I took her throughout the night. My woman is insatiable, and I'm damn lucky to be the one to meet every single one of her needs.

"Landon," she moans, wrapping her legs around my hips and rubbing her pussy up and down my length.

"Yeah, baby?" I groan into her mouth before slipping my tongue inside. I kiss her with long, languid strokes of my tongue, coaxing her to open up wider for me so I can taste more of her. We're both panting by the time I break the kiss.

"More," she whispers against my lips.

"I fucking love you," I growl, possessiveness taking hold of me as I crash my mouth down on hers. I kiss her forcefully, demanding her to understand the depths of my devotion to her. Zoe kisses me right back, searing me with her passion.

"You love me," she murmurs when we finally come up for air. It's not so much a question as a statement to herself.

"I love you with everything I am," I murmur, releasing her hands and kissing her softly before resting my forehead on hers.

"Show me," Zoe says, her other-worldly blue eyes pleading with me to prove my words.

I kiss her slowly, deeply, infusing my words into her with each stroke. Breaking the kiss, I crawl down her body, trailing lips over her creamy skin and soft curves. When I finally reach her center, I nuzzle into her soaking wet pussy.

"Jesus," I groan, unable to resist the urge to lick her from bottom to top. My girl is fucking delicious and I'll never get enough of her.

"More," she whimpers again, more urgently this time.

I growl into her cunt, then scrape my teeth along her clit. She lifts her hips and spreads her legs wider. I press my tongue against her tight as fuck entrance, groaning when I feel her little hole pulse and release a shot of cream into my mouth.

Zoe lets out a pained cry as she rubs her pussy against my face, coating me in her juices. That's my tipping point. Knowing she marked me, that she's as desperate and needy as I am, and that I'm the only one who can satisfy her, has me nearly snarling and gnashing my teeth with a primal need to claim her over and over.

My greedy girl whimpers and reaches out for me as I crawl up her sexy as fuck body. I groan when I feel her delicate fingers trail over my shoulders, my chest, my abs, then lower. Resting my forehead on hers, I hiss out a breath when she wraps her hand around my cock and strokes me up and down.

"Fuck, angel. You feel so good, baby. So damn good." I let her touch me and explore what now belongs to her. Zoe guides me to her entrance and lifts her hips, nudging just the tip inside her wet heat. Her pussy spasms, massaging the head of my cock. "Need me to show you how much I love you?" I ask, pushing in a little further.

"Please," she moans, her fingers curling around my biceps as she spreads her legs open wider for me.

"Need me to make this pussy come? Need me to fill you up so you can fucking come all over me again and again?"

"Yes!" Zoe cries out, thrusting her hips up, taking more of me.

I grunt and pull out, swallowing down her whimpers before shoving my cock all the way inside of her tight little channel. Zoe moans and her pussy flutters around me, coating me with more of her cream.

I pull out, looking down between us as I set a steady pace. "Look at us, angel. Fucking look at your little pussy stretching around me, taking my cock like a good girl."

Zoe whimpers and squeezes her inner muscles, making me growl as every part of my dick throbs in sweet, painful pleasure. "More," she cries out, her lips seeking mine. She owns this kiss, nipping at me and sucking my tongue inside her mouth as her pussy sucks my cock deeper, deeper, so damn deep.

I pull out and slam back inside, swallowing down her cries. God, I can feel her channel stretch and clench around me as I pick up speed. Her legs wrap around my torso, her heels digging into my ass, urging me on.

"Fuck, Zoe. I'm addicted to every part of you," I grit out. I keep hammering into her over and over, tilting my hips and scraping my cock along her front wall in search of...

"Landon!" Zoe shouts and claws at my back, clinging to me as I tear her apart. I can't stop. I know I should slow down. Her pussy has to be sore from all the times we've made love in the last few hours. But I don't have control over anything anymore. My hands slip under her back and slide up, my fingers curling around her shoulders, giving me more leverage to fuck that tight little pussy.

Every time I hit the end of her, Zoe jerks beneath me, letting out the sexiest whimper. I keep pounding into her as I bury my face into the side of her neck, sucking on her soft skin. I feel her entire body tighten around me, her muscles tensing, her pussy throbbing, pulsing, gushing for me.

I grunt with each savage stroke, more beast than man at the moment. I feel her breaking apart for me, her jagged cries and desperate moans growing louder by the second. She bows her back and digs her fingernails into my shoulders, sucking in a huge breath of air. Zoe freezes, tenses, trembles...

And then fucking shatters so beautifully for me.

Her cries of pleasure echo around the room as her cunt snaps around me over and over. I sit back and grip her hips, fucking myself with her spasming pussy. My angel fists the comforter and thrashes her head back and forth as another orgasm rips through her body, leaving her breathless.

"Goddamn," I snarl, shoving my cock deep inside her and staying still. I tip my head back and feel, just fucking feel every ounce of her pleasure ripple around me.

She's still twitching and whimpering out the last of her release when I pull out of her and grab my dick, stroking myself roughly. The need to mark her is such a primal, caveman thing, but it can't be denied. It won't.

My orgasm slams into me, and I roar as I paint her tits and pussy with my cum. I grunt something unintelligible, squeezing my dick so damn hard as it jerks and empties more of my release all over her.

I'm about to collapse, but then my dirty girl rubs my seed into her skin. She cups her breast, pinching her nipple as her other hand trails lower, gathering up my cum before she dips her fingers into her pussy.

"Jesus Christ," I growl, my body shaking with how turned on I still am, despite the intense, all-consuming orgasm I just had.

"Landon," Zoe cries out. "God, Landon, I can't stop, I can't stop." Christ, she fucks her own hand while I hover over her, taking in this goddess. Her mouth opens in a silent scream, all the breath leaving her lungs as she comes again.

I swat her hand away, sliding down her body and prying her legs open. Flattening my tongue, I lick her up and down in frantic, feral strokes before spearing my tongue inside her entrance, scooping out more of her cream.

Zoe winds her fingers in my hair, holding me still as she rubs her pussy against my lips and tongue. Her scream carves through the air as a fierce orgasm overwhelms her tiny body. I grip her thighs, pinning them down to the mattress as I drink down every last drop of her release.

I only stop when she goes completely limp. Looking up from between her legs, I see her head loll to the side as her chest heaves up and down. I crawl up her body, placing kisses on her breasts, neck, and finally her lips.

Collapsing beside her, I drape my angel over my chest and hold her trembling body close. We're both breathing heavily, our bodies slick with sweat as we cling to each other. I comb my fingers through her damp hair and place a kiss on top of her head.

"You okay, love?" I whisper, tugging on her hair slightly to tilt her head up.

"Hmm?" she asks in a daze, her eyelids barely fluttering open as a sleepy, contented smile stretches across her lips.

I grin and kiss the tip of her nose. "Never mind. I've got you," I murmur, tucking her head under my chin. I hold her for long moments, listening to her breaths slowly return to normal. "Do you believe me now?" I finally ask.

"About what?"

"About how much I love you. About how perfect you are. How perfect *we* are."

"You're perfect," she says, her voice so quiet I almost don't hear her. There's a sadness in her tone, one I wish I could take away. I know it will take time though.

"So are you. You're perfect for me, angel. One day you'll believe me about that, too."

Zoe doesn't say anything, she just snuggles closer, like she's trying to dissolve into me. I don't mind. I let her cling to me, willing my strength to cover her and whatever insecurities she has about us. Now that I have her in my arms, I'm never letting her go.

***

I can't believe what I'm seeing.

I rub my eyes and look at my computer screen again, willing the image to be different, the name to be different, something, *anything* to indicate Zoe, *my* Zoe isn't the same woman staring back at me. But no, there it is again, a warrant for her arrest in bold letters.

Zoe Mendoza

Sex: F
Age: 20
Eye Color: Blue
Height: Approx. 5'3"
Last seen in Middleton, Minnesota on February 12th. Wanted for grand theft auto, assault with a deadly weapon, and vandalism resulting in $5,000 of property damage.

What the fuck?

I'm shocked, angry, and hurt. Could it be true? Why didn't she tell me? What is she running from? It's hard to believe the woman I've spent the last week with—the woman I made love to just a few short hours ago—could be the same woman accused of these serious crimes. Like, prison time serious. I may have gotten her out of a fine and a night in the holding cell for trespassing on Mr. Leroy's property, but I don't have the kind of power to get her off the hook for this.

Long moments pass where I'm just staring at the screen, scrolling through the stills from the CCTV cameras she was caught on. It looks like Zoe drove a beat-up old car half way across the country until it broke down outside of Middleton, the next town over. The car was found abandoned on the side of a back country road, covered in snow.

I start to get a clearer picture of what happened before I found Zoe. The car must have broken down, forcing her to walk to the nearest town—Still Creek. For the millionth time since Zoe came into my life, I wonder what she's running from.

It was almost impossible leaving Zoe this morning, especially after I told her I loved her. I knew she wasn't ready to say it back, but I needed her to know where I stood. That hasn't changed, but I'm not sure how to reconcile the soft, sweet woman I held in my arms a few hours ago with the woman I'm looking at on the screen.

I want to understand her, to understand her fear and what danger she found herself in that she felt she had to commit some serious crimes to escape. That has to be why she did it. There's no way my angel is a manipulative, dangerous criminal.

Then again, isn't that exactly what a manipulative, dangerous criminal would want you to think?

I banish that thought as soon as it forms. No way. My cop instincts are on high alert, trying to figure her out and fit her to the crimes she's committed. But another part of me, one I've only recently discovered, takes over. Despite the overwhelming evidence of her crimes—the title of her vehicle registered to someone else, the charges filed against her for assault, the photos of a trailer with broken windows and fire damage—I know there's more to the story.

Suddenly I remember the conversation we had right before I left for work. Zoe said she was feeling cooped up after spending a week inside my house. I suggested she take a walk down Main Street, where there are boutique shops, restaurants, and the best coffee shop in town.

As confused and hurt as I am that she didn't tell me any of her past, I still only want to protect her. If she's out there on the streets, one of my deputies could pick her up. We all get emails about wanted criminals who could potentially be in the area. Still Creek doesn't see much criminal action, so whenever one of these emails comes our way, the deputies are always eager to jump on the case.

I hop up from my desk, not bothering to grab my coat as I run out to my cruiser. If anyone is going to find her and bring her in, it's going to be me. I can't harbor a fugitive, but I can hear her out before she gets interrogated. I can try and help her to the best of my ability. We'll hire the best lawyer and fight for a reduced sentence. I can tell her I love her again and reassure her we'll get through this.

I'm nearly choking on the desperate need to hold her as she tells me her secret pain. Ripping the car door open, I take a deep breath, trying to get my hands to stop shaking long enough to get the car started.

I've only made it two blocks away from the station before my worst nightmare comes true.

"Sheriff Coleman, this is Officer Prescott. We've apprehended Zoe Mendoza and brought her into the station, over."

"Where is she?" I bark. "Over," I grunt after a second of dead air.

"In one of the holding cells. I'm about to call the Middleton police to inform them—"

"No," I nearly shout, the sound leaving my chest in a forceful growl. "Let me talk to her first. Over."

There's another heavy silence, this one stretching on for several seconds before I get a confused but deferential response. "Roger that, Sheriff. She's here. Over and out."

I don't bother with a response as I turn the car around and head back to the station. I'm not a religious man, but I'm praying to every god I can think of that we somehow find a way out of this.

Chapter 8

Zoe

I curl up on the plastic mattress in my holding cell, facing the wall and trying not to cry. This morning, the kindest, strongest, sexiest man alive told me he loved me... and now I'm waiting to be interrogated and probably sent back home to go on trial for my crimes.

I knew my past would catch up to me eventually, I just wish I had longer to hold on to the fantasy. I wish I told Landon I loved him, too, but I couldn't find the words this morning. I think I've loved him since he first put me in handcuffs.

A dry, humorless laugh escapes my lips, followed by a single tear dripping down my cheek. I'm guessing he won't feel the same way now that I'm about to be locked up for a long time.

Some small part of me hoped beyond hope my stepdad would let me go in peace. I left almost two weeks ago and hadn't heard anything from him since that awful night. The bigger part of me knew things were always going to end this way—me, alone, sobbing in a jail cell.

I squeeze my eyes shut, trying to hold onto the memory of being safe in Landon's arms. Tears stream down my face as I wrap my arms around myself to keep from breaking apart completely. He made me feel so treasured, so loved, so absolutely adored... and now I'll never see him again. Of all the losses I've taken in the last decade, that one hits me the hardest.

Burying my head in my hands, I let it all out. I grieve for the little girl who lost her mother all too young. I grieve for the things she had to see, the way she had to grow up, and the impossible decisions she had to make. I grieve for the life I'll never have, the one Landon showed me briefly these last few days.

I'll treasure every sweet word, every gentle touch, every patient gaze for the rest of my life. Those memories will have to get me through somehow. Landon didn't know it at the time, but he was giving me a lifetime supply of love and affection in just the short week we were together.

When I'm all cried out, I wipe my tear-stained face on the scratchy fabric of the sheets. I allow myself one more moment of make-believe, where I'm surrounded by Landon's warm embrace, my face buried into the side of his neck while he holds me and tells me I'm safe. I swear I can even smell his unique clean and smoky scent.

"Zoe?"

My eyes snap open and I scramble up from the fetal position, turning to face the door of the cell. Pain rips through my chest, leaving a throbbing ache I can feel everywhere. Landon slides the door open, standing just inside the small cell.

He should be pissed. Why isn't he pissed? Why do his eyes look as haunted as mine? He shouldn't be here. I wanted my last memory of Landon to be him kissing me roughly and then so sweetly before tucking me back in bed and leaving for work. Now my last memory will be of his disappointment or God forbid, his pity.

"Angel?" Landon asks again, tentatively. "Were they rough with you? Are you cold? Thirsty?"

I shake my head no, trying to will the tears away. Even now, Landon wants me to be safe and comfortable. I was so lucky to have him for any amount of time. In another life, I would have liked to spend the rest of my days thanking him and showing him how much I love him.

"Talk to me," he murmurs, taking a step closer. My heart hammers in my chest, my entire body trembling with the need to launch myself into his arms. But I can't. I have no right to him. Not anymore.

Landon reaches out for me, but I flinch away from his hand, folding in on myself and huddling against the wall. I hate the pain that flashes in his eyes like he needs me as much as I need him. That's not possible. I almost forgot these last few days that I'm trash and I'll always be trash. Now Landon knows it, too.

"Zoe, please, just…" Landon sighs and combs his fingers through his short, dark hair. "I can't help if you don't give me something to work with. I'm not here on official business, not yet, anyway. I'm here as the man who loves you, who needs to protect you."

I want to shout at him to leave me alone, that I'm no good for him, and if he's smart, he'd turn around and never look back. I also want to spill my heart, my secrets, my past to the only man who's ever cared about me. I want to tell him I love him, that I'll love him until my dying breath.

But I don't say any of that.

Instead, I turn toward the wall, giving him my back. It's not fair to make him carry my burdens, just like it's not fair for me to confess my feelings for him. I can't give Landon hope. I can't give myself hope. There's no future here. He may be playing the hero right now, but soon he'll figure out I'm not worth the heartache and complications.

"Can you look at me, angel?" Landon whispers. I can hear his heart breaking with each word.

My chest grows tight and my throat starts to close, but I breathe through it. The sooner he leaves, the sooner I can put all my walls back up. Vulnerability has no place in the life I now have to lead.

"I can't make you talk to me," he finally says after long moments of silence stretch between us. "But I can remind you of what I told you the first morning you woke up in my home. It was Valentine's Day, remember?" Despite my best efforts, I nod my head, sniffling slightly. "I told you I see forever, right here with you." I cover my mouth with my hand, trying to catch the sob before it escapes. I still can't look at Landon. I know if I do, I'll break completely. "I meant every word, love. I still see forever with you. I don't know what the future holds, but I'm not giving up on you. I'm not giving up on our forever."

Every muscle in my body trembles and tenses as I hold myself back. I feel my heart cracking in two. No, fuck that, it's shattering in my chest, the little pieces breaking apart further and further until all that's left is a pile of dust.

I can't look at him. I can't. I won't. It hurts too much.

"Zoe, I—"

"Sheriff, there's a call for you," one of the other officers says through the door.

"Just a minute," comes Landon's gruff reply.

"I think you'll want to take the call," the other guy replies.

Landon growls then sighs, defeatedly. I can feel his intense, worried, frustrated gaze on my back, but still, I don't turn around.

"I love you, Zoe," he murmurs so quietly I almost don't hear him.

The door slides open and then clicks shut. Landon's footsteps fade down the hall, taking every good part of me with them.

***

I don't know what time it is, only that someone dropped off a tray of food for dinner hours ago. It's still on the floor, completely uneaten. A fluorescent light bulb blinks and sputters above my head, then resumes its incessant buzzing sound.

All day, memories have assaulted me. Both good and bad. Precious and horrifying. Tender and violent. I've slipped in and out of sleep a few times, only to be jarred awake by either a nightmare from my childhood or a beautiful dream from the last week with Landon. It's waking up from the sweet dreams that hurts the most, knowing that will never be my reality.

I hear a shuffling from somewhere down the hall, and then a few muffled voices talking over each other. The heavy footsteps stop in front of the door to my cell. I assume I'm being transferred, or at the very least interrogated. When I was first arrested, I waived my right to a phone call. Who would I call anyway? The arresting officer told me they'd track me down a public defense lawyer before taking me in for questioning, so maybe that's who's coming to visit.

Sighing, I sit up in the cot and swing my legs over to the side, preparing myself for the inevitable.

"Zoe Mendoza?" a tall officer asks me.

"Yes," I say with a nod.

"Come with me."

I do as I'm told, following the officer through the maze of a station. I expect to be dropped off in one of those rooms I've seen on tv with the two-way mirror. Instead, I'm brought to what looks like a waiting room with chairs and a little office area behind a window.

"Here she is, Zoe Mendoza," the tall officer says to a woman behind the window. He nods his head in my direction and then rattles off a number from a sheet of paper he's holding.

The woman gives me a tired smile and hands the man standing next to me a plastic bag of what appears to be full of my clothes, shoes, and other things I had with me when I was arrested.

"I don't understand," I whisper, my voice scratchy from tears and disuse.

"You're being released. All charges have been dropped," the woman says, her voice gentle but just as tired as the rest of her.

"I don't understand," I say again, too shocked to form another response.

"Your ride is here," the officer says. "You'll get all the answers soon enough, I reckon." I look up at the man who brought me here and notice for the first time he has kind, green eyes and a full head of gray hair. I give him a questioning look, but he doesn't offer any more information. Instead, he guides me to the other side of the waiting room and uses a key card to open the door for me.

My head is still spinning when I look up and see Landon. His bloodshot eyes meet mine, the worry and relief I find there causing me to choke out a sob. I don't have any more tears, so it just comes out as a pathetic whimper.

Before I have a chance to ask what he's doing here, I'm wrapped up in his arms. Landon lifts me up off the ground, crushing me into his chest.

"I'm sorry," I squeak out pathetically as I wrap my legs around his massive frame and cling to him with all my strength.

"Shh, baby, there's nothing to apologize for. I've got you."

Landon continues to whisper soothing things as he carries me outside. His deep, reassuring voice wraps around me like a blanket, warm and comforting. I sink into his embrace, burying my face into the side of his neck, just like I was dreaming about earlier. I inhale his grounding scent, still not entirely convinced this isn't another dream.

We've stopped moving and are now standing in front of Landon's car. He doesn't let go of me, however. Landon presses his lips to the top of my head, breathing me in and tightening his hold on me.

"You're safe," he whispers. "I love you so much. I won't let him hurt you ever again." I whimper and nod my head. I don't know how Landon knows about my stepdad or how he got me out of jail, but I trust his promise to love and protect me. "Let's go home, angel."

I nod again, lifting my head slightly to look at him. My Landon. My love. His deep brown eyes shimmer with tears as he kisses my forehead, my nose, and finally my lips.

"Home," I whisper, letting the word sink down into my very soul.

Chapter 9

I somehow managed to untangle Zoe from my arms and get her loaded up in the car. If I could have driven home with her wrapped around me, I would have. I don't know if I can stand to be more than a few feet away from her right now, possibly ever.

When we pull into the driveway, I hop out of the car and rush over to her side, helping her out as well. Zoe looks up at me with those brilliant, deep blue eyes of hers full of such emotion. I see the weight of the day, hell, the weight of her life on her shoulders. It's now my duty and honor to take her anxieties away and make her feel safe and loved always.

Zoe doesn't resist as I scoop her up in my arms. She curls into my chest, letting me carry her through the house, directly to the bathroom. I set her down gently on the counter in the bathroom before turning around and drawing water for a bath.

I feel Zoe wrap her arms around me from behind and bury her face between my shoulder blades. I rest my hands over hers where they are gripping my stomach. Closing my eyes, I tip my head back and take a deep breath.

She's here. She's safe. She's mine.

Christ, the last twelve hours have been the worst of my life. Seeing Zoe curled up in the corner of a jail cell damn near broke me, but I had to be strong for her. I knew she was trying to be tough and push me away, but I saw right through it. My angel was terrified and hurt. As much as I wanted to hold her and soothe her, that's not what she needed. Zoe didn't need my words; she needed my actions. She needed to be back home with me, and I made that happen.

I called in every favor I've accrued since becoming sheriff and racked up a few I'll have to pay back later. I dug into Zoe's past, deeper than anyone else investigating the case ever did. They saw a troubled kid who came from a shitty family and an even shittier trailer park. It was easy and convenient to arrest her and not look into why she did what she did. Zoe never stood a chance against a system so clearly rigged against her.

Until she met me.

A little poking, prodding, and investigating led me to Troy Ackerman, Zoe's stepdad. He's sketchy as fuck, which means he had people who were willing to turn on him for the right price.

"I'm sorry," Zoe whispers, breaking me out of my racing thoughts. She grips me tighter like she's afraid I'm going to leave. My heart aches for her, for everything she's been through.

I turn around, cupping her face in my hands. God, even with red-rimmed eyes, blotchy cheeks, and disheveled hair, my angel is so fucking beautiful. After all she's been through, she's still so sweet. So good. So pure.

"There's nothing to apologize for, love." Zoe opens her mouth to protest, but I silence her by brushing my lips against hers. "Let's wash the day off you," I murmur, kissing her once, twice, three times... and then stepping away. Her mouth follows me like a magnet, making me chuckle. I give her one last kiss before slowly stripping her of her clothes.

I turn the water off and help Zoe into the tub, letting my eyes wander over her soft curves and supple skin. She's so beautiful, so absolutely precious, every inch of her. The realization that I could have lost her hits me square in the chest. I've been so busy running around, researching her waste of fucking space stepdad, and negotiating plea bargains for his lackeys who turned on him, the gravity of the situation didn't sink in until now.

"Landon?" she whispers, her big blue eyes fixed right on me.

"I'm right here, baby," I reply, kneeling down next to the tub and grabbing a washcloth. I load it up with soap and begin washing my angel.

Zoe sighs and lets her eyelids flutter closed. "That feels good," she says softly, her muscles relaxing for the first time in hours. I hum in acknowledgment and continue washing her body, loving the fact that she trusts me like this.

When she's all clean, I help her out of the tub and wrap her in a fluffy towel, kissing the tip of her nose. Zoe smiles, but it doesn't reach her eyes. We have so much to talk about, but I'll be right here, letting her know I love her and want to keep her forever. Soon she'll believe me.

I scoop my woman up in my arms and carry her to bed, right where she belongs. Zoe snuggles in the blankets while I strip down. Her eyes roam up and down my body, making me bite back a groan.

"This isn't about that," I half-whisper, half-growl as I crawl into the bed next to her. "I just need to hold you, to feel your skin against mine, and know you're here."

Tears well up in her eyes as she nods her head. I pull her into my arms, draping her over my chest. Zoe clings to me, burying her face in the side of my neck as I stroke her back lightly.

"How... what... how am I here? What did you do? What do you know?" Her voice is soft, but her heart is pounding away in her chest. I can feel her tensing like she's bracing herself for something.

"I'm not going anywhere," I reassure her. Zoe relaxes ever so slightly, giving me more of her weight as she melts into me. "Why don't you tell me what brought you out here to Still Creek? Tell me about Troy Ackerman."

Zoe flinches at his name. Motherfucker. I know who he is, but I want to hear it from her.

"Troy is my stepdad," she says with a resigned sigh. "My mom married him when I was seven. Before then, she..." Zoe tenses again before she whispers, "she was a prostitute."

"Zoe..." I hold her closer and brush a kiss to the top of her head. I can't imagine growing up like that.

"Anyway," she continues, not wanting to get caught up in the past. I can respect that. We have all the time in the world for her to tell me everything. I'll replace every painful memory with a happy one. "Shortly after their wedding, Mom was diagnosed with breast cancer. Over the next three years, I watched the fight drain from her body. That wasn't the scariest part though." Zoe takes a deep breath and snuggles closer to me as she shows me her vulnerable, tender heart. "The scariest part was watching the fight drain from her eyes. It wasn't just her body giving up, it was her will to live. Her spirit. Her very soul. She died a week after my tenth birthday. She wasn't the most caring mother, but she was mine, you know?"

God, her voice is so small, so tentative. I comb my fingers through her long black hair and kiss the top of her head. "I'm so sorry, love," I murmur.

"I didn't have any other family. Troy never seemed like he wanted kids or liked me very much, but he let me stay with him. The first few months weren't terrible, but..." I tighten my hold on her, pulling her impossibly closer. I know what comes next, and I hate that she was living with that asshole for so long. "The medical bills and funeral costs were out of control. I don't know when it happened, but somehow Troy got into drugs, not just using them but selling as well. Eventually, he started a small operation for cooking meth out of our trailer." A shiver runs through her, breaking my heart. "He said if I didn't help, he'd send me into foster care," she whispers. "He said I was trash and I'd always be trash."

"Baby, no." I cup the back of her neck, tilting her head up so we're face to face. "You are my kind, sweet, beautiful angel. Zoe, you are my whole world. When I look at you, I see a fighter. I see a woman determined to live life on her own terms. I told you, love, I see forever." I kiss her forehead and then tuck her back into my chest where she rests her head.

"After I graduated high school, I got a job as a waitress. I wanted to save up enough money to move out. Troy was pissed when I told him about my job. He said I already had one, cooking meth with him. The next morning when I was getting ready for my first shift, he..." she trembles and folds in on herself as if reliving a terrible memory. "He beat me up pretty bad. Broke my leg and a few ribs. Needless to say, I lost the waitress job. I didn't try to find another one after that."

Jesus fucking Christ.

I clench my teeth and physically force down the growl threatening to burst free. I knew Troy Ackerman was the worst kind of scum, but knowing he laid hands on my angel? That he bruised her delicate skin and snapped her bones? Rage and fierce, primal protectiveness weave their way through my bloodstream, making me shake.

Violent fantasies of ending Troy's life cloud my vision but I take a breath and focus on the present. He's already in custody, along with four other men and one woman. After my unsanctioned investigation, I tipped off the DEA to Troy's meth lab. Zoe will never have to worry about her past coming to haunt her again.

"I'm so sorry you went through that," I whisper. "Never again, angel. No one will ever hurt you again." She nods, then turns her head and presses the sweetest kiss over my heart. "What happened that night two weeks ago?"

"A drug deal gone horribly wrong." I knew that much, but it still hurts hearing her say it. I hate that Zoe was caught up in that dark world for so long. How the hell did she stay so sweet? "We were cooking a batch of meth when some guys started pounding on the door of the trailer. I don't know what happened first or how things escalated so quickly, but shots rang out, and then there was just chaos. I don't know how else to describe it."

Zoe shivers in my arms, reliving the horrors of that day. She drags in a ragged breath as tears clog her throat.

"You're safe now, baby. I've got you. Take your time," I whisper. She nods, burying her face into the side of her neck as tears wet my skin.

"Somewhere between crouching on the kitchen floor and fighting off one of the guys who stormed our trailer, I snapped," she whispers. "I couldn't do it. I couldn't live like that for a single second longer. I knew where Troy kept the guns, and I managed to slip past the brawl in the living room and grab one from his bedroom."

Zoe adjusts herself so she's propped up on her elbow, facing me. I watch, mesmerized, as the fear and sadness in her eyes are overtaken by pride and determination. I want to always see her like this—strong, brave, and self-assured.

"What happened next?" I gently prod.

"I honestly don't know how I did what I did. I swear I was floating above it all somehow, watching myself do these things I never thought I'd be brave enough to do. I knocked over the propane tanks we used for cooking, which started a fire. Troy grabbed me, but it was the last time I'd let him put his fucking hands on me." She's talking fast now, her words running together as she gets out all of the gritty details. "I hit him with the butt of the gun and then shot his leg. I don't remember what happened after, just that I hopped in Troy's car and kept driving, driving, driving..."

"You were driving home, love," I whisper into the shell of her ear before kissing her temple. I nuzzle into the side of her neck, placing a soft kiss there, trying to calm her down and bring her back into the present moment. "You were driving straight to me."

Zoe nods, turning her head and capturing my lips with hers. She gives me everything in this one kiss. My angel poured out her heart and soul, and now she's surrendering to my love and care.

I cup the side of her face, drawing her closer as my other hand trails down her back. Zoe moans, rubbing her naked body against mine. Her kiss turns desperate, her tongue lashing against mine, her fingernails clawing at my chest. Zoe straddles my hips, this beautiful, broken goddess on display just for me.

She leans down and crashes her mouth over mine. I let her take what she needs, meeting her stroke for stroke as she grinds her pussy against my bare cock. Zoe lets out a strangled moan that almost sounds like she's crying.

I cup the back of her neck, stilling her movements and guiding her to rest her forehead on mine. She's shaking, still clawing at me, like she needs this closeness, needs every part of me. Fuck, I need it, too.

I nuzzle into the side of her neck and then flip Zoe over on her back, kissing away her gasp of surprise. Settling between her legs, I gather up her wrists in one of my hands before pinning them above her head.

Bending down, I ghost my lips down her neck, her collarbone, her chest, until I get to her breasts. I rub my nose over one nipple and then take it in my mouth. Zoe whimpers and bucks her hips to get me where she wants me.

"Slow down," I whisper before kissing the hollow of her neck. "I will fuck you hard and deep when you need it, but right now, I need to show you you're worth taking time on." I kiss up her neck and jaw until my lips are inches from hers. "Let me savor you, angel. Let me love you like this."

She nods, tears glistening in her eyes.

I release her hands and sit back on my heels so I can map out her body with my fingers. Slowly, I trace a line down her neck, her shoulders, the inside of her arm. I draw circles on the tender flesh of her wrists where I feel her pulse pounding against the pads of my fingers.

Continuing my survey, my hands wander to her breasts, cupping one in each hand and bending down to kiss the tops and place open-mouthed kisses in the valley in between. I lick the sensitive underside of one breast and then the other. Zoe shudders at my touch.

I nip and kiss and lick at the soft, delicate skin on her torso, lavishing every inch of her with my love and adoration. There isn't a single part of this magnificent body I don't love.

I scoot down the bed until her sweet pussy is right in front of my face. Throwing one leg over my shoulder and then the other, I scoop her ass up and bring her closer to me. I can't hold back any longer, her scent calling out to me, beckoning me to have a taste.

I swipe my tongue into her slit and groan when I find her already dripping for me. I bury my face into her cunt, spearing my tongue in her entrance and swirling my nose around her little bundle of nerves. Licking up her slit, I take my time rubbing slow, lazy circles on the outside of her sensitive clit, never quite touching her where she needs. Zoe whimpers, her delicious sounds only encouraging me to draw this out.

I growl into her soaking folds and relish the way her entire body trembles, more tortured moans falling from her precious lips. Finally, I suck on her clit, pulling it between my lips and swiping my tongue over the pulsing bundle again and again.

"Landon, oh God, don't... don't stop," she moans, her voice cracking as her breath gets stuck in her throat.

I slide my right hand down from where I've been gripping her ass and thrust two fingers into her sopping wet pussy. It makes the most satisfying smacking sound as I pump in and out of her while continuing my assault on her clit.

I feel her pulsing, tensing, winding up for me. One scrape of my teeth over her clit and my angel explodes for me, twisting and crying out as I hold her steady. I replace my fingers with my tongue, dipping it into her gushing entrance and scooping out her juices, drinking down everything she's giving me.

When I'm sure I've wrung out everything I can from her, I tear my face away from the most decadent meal I've ever had in my life. Looking up at Zoe from between her legs, I see her chest heaving and her rosy cheeks flushed from her orgasm. She lets out a little breathy sigh each time she exhales like the pleasure is too much to be silent. It makes me fucking roar inside with pride.

I crawl up her body, placing wet kisses on her thighs, her breasts, her neck, until finally, I take her lips in a slow, sensual kiss.

When we come up for air, I line myself up with her entrance and look into those gorgeous eyes of hers. She looks at me with trust, love, and adoration. It means every-fucking-thing to me to see her look at me like that after everything we've been through today.

"Ready for more, love?" I ask.

"Please..." she whispers.

Slowly, so slowly, I slide inside her warmth. Inch by inch, I feel her stretching for me, her walls pulsing and sucking me deeper inside of my new home. When I finally hit the end of her, we both let go of a breath. Staying completely still, I memorize the way her pussy feels wrapped around me.

I rest my forehead on hers, needing Zoe to feel this with me. I gently suck her top lip in between mine in a soft kiss and then switch to her bottom lip. I keep nipping at her sweet, pouty lips while filling her up with every inch of me.

Zoe winds her arms around my neck and slides her fingers into my hair, pulling me in to deepen the kiss. I start rocking in and out of her as our tongues tangle together. She breaks the kiss to suck in air, and I take the opportunity to nuzzle and kiss her neck, licking her pulse point and feeling her heartbeat under my lips, my tongue.

I keep a steady pace as she meets me thrust for thrust. Without warning, I flip us over so she's on top. I pull her down so we're chest to chest, the angle allowing me to wedge myself so deep inside her I fucking see stars. I grit my teeth to keep from coming.

"Oh, God, it's... Landon, you're so deep..."

Her hips twitch and buck and she cries out as my cock scrapes against her G-spot again and again. I cup her ass and drag her body up and down, giving us both the friction we need. It's a slow, intense burn, one that has us both gasping each time I hit the end of her.

Zoe buries her head in my neck as her legs tighten around me. I grip her ass harder, shoving her tight little cunt down my cock as far as she can take it. My angel comes so hard, convulsing in my arms and sobbing out her release. I feel her juices gush all over me as her pussy throbs. I fuck her through it, feeling the tender, swollen flesh of her pussy pulse around me again and again.

I wrap my arms around her back, keeping her body flush against mine as my hips snap and pump into her. Zoe lifts her head up, resting her forehead on mine. Her entire body jerks in my arms as she comes again.

Her pussy knots around me, the muscles coiling like cords to secure me inside of her. We grind our bodies together, circling, pulling, pushing, each motion lodging me deeper. I feel her little body trembling as she struggles through another intense orgasm.

"Hold me tight, love," I tell her, kissing down her neck and back up again, brushing my lips against her ear. "Don't let me go, stay with me, love, stay right here with me..."

She crushes her lips on mine and I taste the salt of her tears as we both kiss and cry and melt into each other with every thrust. Zoe moans into my mouth as she comes one last time, taking me with her over the edge.

I swell inside her as my orgasm shoots down my spine, drawing my balls up tight and then emptying into her with such force I think I might pass out. I keep coming inside of her, my dick raw and throbbing as I empty myself over and over. I've never come so hard for so long.

When I'm finally done, I stroke Zoe's back. She's a pile of bones on top of me, completely spent. Every few seconds, she shudders out another wave of pleasure and whimpers softly into my chest where her head is resting.

We stay like that for minutes, hours, God knows how long. I feel myself growing hard again, my cock still buried deep inside of her. Zoe moans and pushes herself up on her knees and begins to ride me.

"Jesus, fuck, Zoe..." I grit out as I grab her hips and help her set a steady rhythm.

She rolls her body on top of mine, digging her nails into my chest as she uses me to get herself off. I'm reminded of that first morning I woke up to her little body wrapped around me, how she craved my touch even in her sleep, even before she really knew me. Watching Zoe writhe on top of me, now, her tits jiggling, her chest heaving with every breath as she cries out her pleasure... It's all too much for me to take.

I reach out and rub her clit in furious circles, needing her to get there before I fill her up with my cum again. Zoe's arms buckle underneath her, and she falls to my chest. I flip us over and throw both of her legs over one of my shoulders, thrusting my hard cock inside of her and pounding into her at this new angle.

"Goddamn, baby, you're so fucking tight like this," I growl.

Zoe fists the sheets and thrashes her head back and forth, bowing her back off the mattress. I slap her ass and piston in and out of her.

"Landon, Landon... right there, yes, yes..."

She screams as her pussy chokes my dick, making me pump into her one last time and then explode with a roar.

I reluctantly pull out and set her legs down before collapsing next to her. We're both panting and sweating. After a few minutes of calming down, Zoe shuffles over to me and I tuck her into my side, kissing her forehead and holding her tightly against me.

"Are you okay, baby?" I ask.

"Mmhmm. So good," she breathes out.

I smile at her sleepy response.

Zoe pops her little head up off of my chest and hits me deep with her deep blue eyes. It's a look I can't quite place.

Before I can spiral too far, Zoe presses a kiss on my forehead and the tip of my nose.

"I love you," she whispers.

I close my eyes, breathing in her words. "Tell me again," I say so softly I don't know if she even heard.

"I love you, Landon. Thank you for seeing something in me, something worth protecting and loving. I didn't know I could feel like this." Zoe looks away from me, her cheeks stained the lightest pink.

"Like what?" Zoe shrugs, but I'm not letting her get shy on me now. "How do I make you feel?"

"Adored. You make me feel so precious and adored."

Goddamn, this woman and her clear blue eyes and pure soul.

"You are, angel. You are both of those things and so much more. You've got a beautiful heart, Zoe, and I think I'd like to keep it."

She smiles at me, the sparkle in her eyes making it hard to breathe. She's so fucking it for me. "Only if I get to keep yours, too."

"Don't you know? It was yours from the moment I saw you. But if you want to make it official..."

I gently roll Zoe on her side so I can reach over and grab something from the side table drawer. She gives me a questioning look, then gasps when she sees the ring box I have in my hand. I open it and slide the diamond ring on her finger, not giving her a chance to say no.

"Landon..." Her eyes dart from the ring to my face, then back to the ring. "Well, are you going to ask me?"

I bark out a laugh and then flip her on her back, swallowing down her squeal of surprise in an all-consuming kiss.

"Will you be mine?" I murmur into the shell of her ear.

"Will I be your what?" she teases nipping my earlobe. I love this feisty side of her. I hope to bring out more of it.

"Everything, angel. I want you to be my everything. My best friend, my wife, the mother of my children. I'll give you everything, all of me in return. But make no mistake, love. This is forever. We're forever."

"Just like you're always saying," she whispers, tears glistening in her eyes.

"Is that a yes?"

Zoe nods her head enthusiastically, brushing her nose against mine. The sweetest giggle falls from her lips. I have to taste it for myself. My angel opens up for me, letting me drink her down. I vow to always make her feel this loved. From this day forward, Zoe will always know how much I adore her.

Epilogue

"Mommy, Mommy, Mommy, wake up!"

I pop one eye open, looking at my beautiful baby girl. Alison turned six last month, and she's such a little ray of sunshine. Her bright blue eyes sparkle as she gives me a toothy smile.

"Morning, sweetheart. What's—"

Alison tugs at my arm before I can finish my thought. "Come *on*!" she urges, making me laugh. I throw on a robe and my slippers and follow her out into the kitchen.

"Happy Valemtimes Day, Mom!" Aaron, our four-year-old shouts. He has a too-large apron tied around him with food spills all over it.

"What's going on?" I ask, looking around the disaster area that is my kitchen.

"You were supposed to go to the dining room so you didn't see the aftermath," Landon says from behind me, wrapping his arms around my waist and kissing my temple. "You look beautiful today, angel."

I know I look like a mess, but I truly believe he thinks I'm beautiful no matter what. My tummy flips every time he calls me angel. Even after seven years of marriage, my husband still has the ability to make me melt with a single word.

Landon guides me to the dining room, chuckling when Alison and Aaron dart ahead of him to sit at the table.

"Oh my gosh, what is all this?" I gasp, looking around at the feast spread out on the table.

"Breakfast, duh," Aaron quips.

"Aaron, what did we say about using that word?" Landon reprimands.

"It's rude," he sighs.

Landon squeezes our son's shoulder reassuringly and kisses him on top of his head. For being a big, bad, tattooed sheriff, he's such a softie when it comes to his family. I'm usually the one doling out punishments. Not that I need to very often. Our kids are so sweet and thoughtful, just like their dad.

"Eggs benedict, fresh fruit and yogurt parfait, coffee, juice, and bacon for good measure," Landon continues, answering my question.

"You made eggs benedict?" I ask in shock. "Bold move."

He chuckles and pulls out my chair for me, helping me get settled. These sweet little gestures do me in every time. I'm reminded every day how lucky I am to keep this man for the rest of my life.

"I had some help." Landon nods to our kids, who are waiting impatiently for us to start breakfast.

"Thank you, everyone. This is such a lovely way to start the day." I squeeze Alison's hand and then Aaron's, trying not to cry. I never imagined my life would turn out this way. I still think about those horrible few hours I spent in that jail cell, thinking I'd never see Landon again. And here I am, sharing a meal prepared by my family for me on Valentine's Day.

Landon cups the side of my face, tilting my head up to meet his gaze. "Happy Valentine's Day, love," he murmurs before bending down and taking my lips in a soft kiss.

"Ew!" Alison squeals.

Landon chuckles, the deep sound vibrating through me. He gives me one last kiss and takes his seat next to me.

The four of us laugh and talk about the day ahead as we devour the delicious breakfast. Landon has gotten better at cooking over the years, though I never cease to poke fun at him for his first failed attempt at making a meal. I also make sure to tell him that was part of the reason I fell for him so hard and fast. It was endearing watching him flounder and stumble over his words trying to impress me. Not that he needed to try hard. Everything about Landon called out to every part of me. It still does.

When Landon came to my rescue seven years ago, I had no plan except get the hell out of Dodge. My life up until that point had been about surviving. I didn't have the luxury of dreaming about the future when the present was an all-consuming battle every day. But Landon was so patient with me, encouraging me to explore my interests and take time to figure out what I wanted out of life.

When I decided to illustrate children's books, he didn't bat an eyelash at my impractical career choice. I was nervous to show him my sketches, but of course, he praised me endlessly and told me how proud he was of me. Together, we navigated the world of children's books and found authors looking for illustrators. My first book was published five years ago, and Landon likes to remind me he was my first and biggest fan.

"What are you thinking about, angel?" Landon asks softly, his warm brown eyes meeting mine across the table.

"Just how wonderful you are to me," I answer honestly. He grins, pride shining in his eyes. I know what he's thinking. He's proud to be the man who gets to love me for the rest of my life. He tells me so all the time.

After breakfast, the kids dash off to their rooms to get ready for the day. I start clearing up the dishes, but Landon stops me with a hand on the small of my back.

"I'll take care of cleaning up. I have another surprise for you," he murmurs, kissing the side of my neck. I bite my bottom lip and look at him over my shoulder. Landon groans and presses a chaste kiss on my lips. "How is everything you do the sexiest goddamn thing?"

Before I can answer, my big, burly husband scoops me up in his arms and carries me to our room. I giggle and wrap my arms around his neck, kissing his chin. Landon closes the door with his foot and sets me down, pressing me against the wall.

The heat and hunger in his eyes send a shiver down my spine, but it's the love and adoration underneath that warms me up. He's always looking at me like that, and it never gets old.

Dipping his head down, Landon trails his lips up my neck, kissing and nipping at my pulse point. "As much as I want to fuck you right up against this wall, I don't want to scar our children for life."

I huff out a laugh, then moan as he grinds his thick cock into my stomach. Landon threads his fingers through my hair, tipping my head up and crashing his mouth down on mine. I immediately open up for him, sliding my tongue against his and getting lost in his kiss. One after another, he bombards me with kisses, each one rougher, needier than the last.

I'm a panting, whimpering mess by the time he finally pulls away.

Landon rests his forehead on mine breathing me in. "Damn, woman," he whispers. "I'll never get enough of you. He surprises me by wrapping me up in his arms and rocking me back and forth. This man. He's equal parts sexy, insatiable beast, and sweet, caring protector.

"You said there was another surprise?" I ask once he steps away. Landon grins at me and goes to the closet, digging around for something. When he returns, he's holding a box of chocolates and a bouquet of roses.

"A bit cliché, maybe, but a beautiful woman deserves beautiful flowers and chocolate on Valentine's Day."

I smile when I think about that first Valentine's Day we spent together. He told me the same thing. I remember confessing to him that no one had ever gotten me anything before. Since then, Landon has showered me with gifts. Most of the time it's not anything extravagant, just little flowers or notes, but he makes me feel so loved.

"Thank you, husband," I say with a smile as I take the gifts.

Landon draws me in for another hug, candy, flowers, and all. "Love hearing you call me that," he whispers. "Love being your husband."

"I love being your wife," I murmur, kissing his chest right over his heart.

Landon nuzzles into the top of my head, making me smile at his sweet gesture. "I absolutely adore you, Zoe," he says with all the tender conviction in the world.

I soak up all of his love, letting it fill me up. This man has given me more than he could ever know. A life full of joy and laughter, a safe place to regroup, a shoulder to cry on. He's shown me every single day that I'm worthy of him, worthy of a happily ever after. It took a little while to undo the lies I was told growing up, but I can't possibly feel like trash when Landon clearly treasures me above everything and everyone else.

Overcome with gratitude, I tilt my head up and kiss him slowly, deeply, before whispering, "I absolutely adore you, too, husband." Landon gives me a heart-stopping smile, rubbing his nose up and down mine.

Our moment is interrupted by the kids bursting into our room.

"Pretty flowers!" Alison gushes.

"Chocolate!" Aaron chimes in.

Landon chuckles, opening the box of chocolates. He hands it to me first, letting me have the first pick. Then he lets the kids take one chocolate each. "Brush your teeth when you're done with your snack," he says, trying to be authoritative. I wait until the kids leave to laugh at him. "What? Something funny?"

I nod. "You when you're trying to be stern."

He narrows his eyes at me, but then grins, kissing me on the tip of my nose. "I can't help it," he says with a shrug. Landon spins me around and gives my ass a playful smack. "Are you ready to start the day, love?"

I look at him over my shoulder, giving him a sweet smile. "With you? Always."

He returns my smile with an even bigger one. "Good. You're stuck with me now, angel. I'm yours forever."

"Forever," I confirm, blinking back tears. I don't know if Valentine's Day miracles exist, but Landon is mine. My miracle, my valentine, my husband. My forever.

***

THE END

Want more protective alphas & sweet heroines? Check out my popular bodyguard series, Watchdog Protection, Inc.[1]!

---

1. *https://books2read.com/u/bOj5JA*

Also by Cameron Hart

Check out my other popular series and books!
Mafia, MC, & Bodyguard Romance:
<u>Moscatelli Crime Family Series</u>[2]
<u>Di Salvo Crime Family Series</u>[3]
<u>Chaos MC series</u>[4]
<u>Savage Ride</u>[5]
Mountain Man Romance:
<u>Men of Blackthorne Mountain Series</u>[6]
<u>Bear's Tooth Mountain Men Series</u>[7]
Cowboy & Small Town Romance:
<u>Roped in by Love Series</u>[8]

2. https://books2read.com/u/mqBaze

3. https://books2read.com/u/m0odzW

4. https://books2read.com/u/bMVAOk

5. https://books2read.com/u/bMVlG7

6. https://books2read.com/u/3RYDvB

7. https://books2read.com/u/mVel7A

8. https://books2read.com/u/3RYlBY